Girl in Red

Gaye Hiçyılmaz is the author of a number of highly praised novels for children and young adults, published by Faber and Dolphin. Her Dolphin titles (published under the name Annie Campling) are *And the Stars Were Gold* and *Smiling for Strangers*.

Gaye Hiçyılmaz grew up in England but then spent twenty years living in Turkey and Switzerland. She has three sons and a daughter all now grown up, and she lives with her partner on the Pembrokeshire coast, where she writes overlooking the sea.

Also by Gaye Hîçyılmaz

(first published under the name of Annie Campling)

And the Stars Were Gold
Smiling for Strangers

Girl in Red

Gaye Hiçyılmaz

Dolphin Paperbacks

First published in Great Britain in 2000
as a Dolphin paperback
by Orion Children's Books
a division of the Orion Publishing Group Ltd
Orion House
5 Upper St Martin's Lane
London WC2H 9EA

Reprinted 2001, 2002

A catalogue record for this book is available
from the British Library

ISBN 1 85881 490 1

Typeset at The Spartan Press Ltd,
Lymington, Hants

Printed in Great Britain by
Clays Ltd, St Ives plc

For Hülâgü Hasan:
thank you for
all your help

1

....

Friday 13 November 1998

'They're back again!' Ian is snatching a quick smoke on the balcony outside. He leans over the wet rail to peer at something I can't see.

'Yea?' I make my answer sound casual: interested but not too keen. That's the right note to sound with Ian Bresslaw. He expects people to be interested in him.

'Just *look* at them!' He leans over even further and shakes his head tolerantly. When he turns back to us he's smiling to himself and there's a straight, damp line on his shirt. It runs across his stomach.

He's an amazingly tall man, and thin, and even though I don't think he's that great, I don't like seeing him standing so near that wet edge. He's leaning over too far. After all, he's a good friend of Mum's and a lot better than some of her boyfriends have been. But I'm still not tempted to get up from the armchair, *my* armchair, actually, to join him. I know exactly what will happen if I do. As soon as I'm out there on the balcony he'll be telling me things and I'll be listening. Then, just when he's got me thinking about something, he'll take another quick drag, stub out the butt on the rail and slide back into the sitting-room in front of me. Then he'll sit in my armchair. I'll either be left out in the rain on the balcony or I'll have to sit on the sofa beside Lucy, who'll wriggle closer and show me stupid things in magazines.

I know she's only trying to be friendly, but Lucy Bresslaw must be the most boring girl in the world. I've never wanted to coo over pictures of puppies in baskets and I'm not going to just because Mum says we have to be nice to her. She's a bore, which is odd because her dad, Ian, isn't. Not if I'm honest.

Far, far away and almost on the horizon, one of the car ferries from Dover is moving through grey seas in the low autumn sun. Normally, I wouldn't have minded leaning on the rail and watching for a bit, even if it is raining, but I'm not letting old Ian get my armchair. Not yet, anyway.

Then we hear raised voices. Lucy smoothes out the folded corner of a page that she must have looked at a hundred times already. It's Liz Quiggley from the ground floor. You'd know her voice anywhere. One of her sons, Sam, is in my class, but luckily the Quiggley voice must have skipped a generation. Things do that, you know, like pop-eyes in my family. My grandad was quite a bug, judging by his photo, and Mum can look a bit froggy, especially first thing in the morning – not that it isn't quite cute, in a way. That's what I tell her, anyway. And it certainly doesn't put blokes off. But I'm not froggy, not even slightly. I'm like my dad, I suppose. I'm cuddly: more teddy-bear than amphibian. So Sam Quiggley must be quiet like *his* dad, whoever that is, and Sam doesn't seem to know any more about it than I do. He just isn't like his mum. Liz Quiggley could scream for England.

2

She admits it herself. She throws her head back and shakes with anger or laughter, like some huge, yellow-toothed horse, up on its hind legs and stuffed into leggings that are too tight.

'Don't mind *me*!' she screams, with a fag flapping about on her bottom lip like something off black-and-white TV. 'Don't mind me, luv, it's just my way. I don't mean nothing by it. I was *born* noisy, I was. It's just the way I am!'

My mum, June, doesn't think much of the way Liz Quiggley is, so I don't go in downstairs, even though Sam and I often walk to school together. You don't need to go into the Quiggleys' flat anyway: the whole block can hear what's happening in there. If, somewhere, deep down below and under all this concrete, there are moles and worms and beetles and stuff creeping around and doing their own silent thing in the tight, dark earth, I bet they shiver and curl up when Liz Quiggley's on the rampage above.

'I said shove off!' That's Liz again and it's quite nice and polite for her.

Lucy sniggers and chews on a bit of hair. Ian slinks back in and I know why: if he'd gawked over that rail any longer Liz might have turned her attentions on him. Effortlessly, and from three floors below, she could have told him to mind his own blinding business and to close his stupid mouth before his useless tongue fell out. Ian's a teacher, a history teacher actually, though luckily not one of mine, and teachers don't like that sort of comment, or not from the other side of their classroom.

'Look you, I *said* shove–' Liz squawks. Ian is struggling with the warped balcony door and a wet, gusty wind. The squeal of the rusty hinge cuts through the rest of her rant.

'What's going on, Dad?' Lucy tilts her good little face up to her father. Her perfectly neat fringe and that helmet of smooth hair fall back into place except for the sticky bit, where she's sucked. I'm always surprised at the way some girls stay so neat and tidy, like kids in picture books.

'It's them again,' says Ian. 'I think it's those travellers we saw earlier. Now it looks as though they're trying to get some old van into the car park. It's causing a bit of a stir, but your neighbour's on the case.'

There's more commotion below. A dog is barking: barking and barking and choking too, as though only just held back. It's suddenly very quiet in our flat, so quiet that I can hear Lucy's fingers on the old creased pages as she tries to smooth them out. Then I remember Mum. She'll be home from work any minute now. It won't be very nice for her, having to cross the car park with that racket going on. She doesn't like upsets. Neither do I, really. Hopefully she'll stop off and do a bit of shopping on the way home. Then she'll miss all this.

I jump up and go to the kitchen to fill the kettle. Mum likes a cup of tea when she gets in and so do I. When I was much younger I always used to do my homework as soon as I got back from school; then I'd start the tea for the two of us. I used to like cooking then. Now everybody's doing it. Sometimes I used to have it all ready before she did her special knock to let me know it was her at the door. She'd step out of her high heels and suddenly look really small as she hung the jacket of her suit on the hanger. Then she'd sit down on her side of the kitchen table. I'd find the oven gloves and reach in. She'd be wriggling the brown, triangular tips of her toes in her tights, to get the

4

circulation going. She'd breathe in the hot smells of whatever I'd put in the stove. She'd say 'mmm . . . ' whatever the dish was, even if it was a bit burnt, which happened sometimes, or was one of my famous made up recipes. Sardines and eggs was one: it makes me want to throw up when I think about it now, but she never ever said a thing. She'd just go 'mmm' and smile and I'd set the dish carefully on the mat, holding tightly, not caring how hot and slippery it was through the glove. She didn't fuss, didn't say 'careful' or 'you'll burn yourself', like other people always do. She'd just wriggle her toes under the table and wait. She knew I could do it.

It's different now. I've got too much homework and she's often quite late back and we both have other stuff to do. And recently, of course, there's been Ian. And Lucy. It's not quite the same, doing things for them. It's not that I don't like them, but four people is a lot more than two, isn't it? And Ian may be as thin as a rake, but my god, you should see him eat! Anyway, I'm fed up with cooking, especially now that other boys cook too.

Ian has switched on the telly. Now he's crossed his long legs. Leaning back in *my* chair, he's fingering the damp patch on his desert boots. I'm surprised he hasn't remembered that Mum is due home. She says he's a real gentleman: he brings flowers and bottles of wine and that sort of thing. And that's another reason why we don't drink so much tea. Nowadays she'll pop out to the supermarket and get something ready cooked, 'to go with a nice bottle of red', or whatever he's brought. And what do I care? It makes my life easier. Actually, I hope that's what she's doing now: reaching into the chill cabinet for a large packet of something

5

spicy and foreign. Last week we had those huge pink prawns, with ginger, I think, and something lemony.

Then I remember the loo window. If I balance on the seat and hold on to the shower rail I can just about see down into the car park. I did this soon after Mum had started going out with Ian. I saw them together in her car and then I wished I hadn't. I'm not a curtain twitcher like Mrs Seagrove in the ground floor flat. I never have been because Mum's always acted really straightforwardly about things like that. She even told me about Brian who was *such* a disaster. Sometimes I think she's too straightforward. I mean, no bloke wants to know *that* much about the men in their mother's life, do they? So I don't spy out of the loo window any more.

But today is different. This is for Mum's own good – and I've lost the armchair anyway. I get the milk out of the fridge and drop a couple of teabags in the pot but I leave the water on. Ian will have to get up and do something once the kettle starts to whistle.

The loo window's stiff too. It's the metal frames and the damp. All the flats are the same: you get disgusting blackish water trickling off the sills in winter. With another jab I force the window back and stick my head out. A gull sails past quite close. It lands, tottering a bit as its orange feet grip the edge of the gutter and the wind and rain gust up. I suspect that it's watching me, but I'm never sure with gulls. There's something about their eggy-yellow beaks with that unexpected curve down at the tip. It gives them a permanent scowl, like old bleached blondes of forty who've finally noticed that nobody's interested in them any longer. I'd never mess with a gull.

There's no sign of Mum. I can't see the whole car park, but I can see our bay and her car isn't there. Mrs Seagrove's new white cat is sitting on the top of the wall just as if it wasn't raining. In the kitchen the kettle is building up to an earsplitting whistle. I used to want a cat, well, a kitten actually, when I was little. But I expect it would have got fleas and shredded things up, because cats do that. Mrs Seagrove's sofa looks like some maniac's been at it with a razor. And as Mum always says: I'll be off in a few more years and what would she do with a cat, all on her own? Once I suggested that a cat would be company for her, but that really upset her and she asked if I thought she was like Mrs Seagrove, who doesn't have any friends. I told her not to be daft but I haven't mentioned cats since.

There's still nothing special to see down below, so maybe Ian got it wrong and it's just an ordinary neighbourhood scrap. He's not from round here, so he does tend to get the wrong end of the stick. The cat jumps down and the gull launches itself off, and poops, so I lean out again, just to see if it lands on anyone. Then I hear a crash. It's glass breaking and the cat's streaking back through Mrs Seagrove's top window. People are yelling, absolutely yelling, and I can hear more banging: bang, bang, bang and glass showering down each time. It's not a break-in, but more like someone doing over a bus shelter, except that there isn't one down there.

Then I catch sight of this girl. She's shuffling backwards. It's as if she's trying to edge away from something with very tiny steps, so that no one will notice. The hem of her skirt, which is much too long, is trailing in the puddles. She doesn't seem to notice, but she's standing there, in the middle of the largest one, so that her shoes must be soaking.

7

Suddenly she bends down and picks something out of the water. I can see the ripples and the drips flying from her hand as she shakes it dry. She's wearing a red skirt, deep, dark red, and darker still at the back where she bent down to the water. I can see her reflection: the red amongst all that wet black.

Mum's car turns in off the road. The girl doesn't move. For one awful moment I think that Mum hasn't seen her, that she'll just swing sharply round like she always does, ready to back into our parking place. The last thing she'll expect is some girl, still as a statue, blocking the way. I call out but it's no use. The kettle's drowning everything anyway, but I still try. Then, with a soft little crunch, the shower rail comes off the wall. There's an avalanche of polyfilla and rattling curtain rings and I pitch awkwardly on to the green tiled floor with one foot still stuck in the loo.

'Frankie?' It's Lucy. 'Frankie?' She's at the bathroom door, turning the knob round and round. I'm crawling out when I notice the blood. It's splashed on the curtain and even up the wall: I've bitten my tongue and right through, by the feel of it.

'Frankie?'

'Turn that kettle off, can't you?' I yell back, spitting into the basin. She doesn't because I can still hear it screaming away.

'Frankie?' I can see her fair hair and her pink lips pressed close to the pebbled glass.

'Frankie? Are you all right?'

'Of course I'm not all right,' I mutter thickly, running the tap on to the red blood. It quivers and streaks into orange and then into yellow and is finally washed away.

2

....

Friday evening

'Oh Francis! Really! How could you?' Now Mum is at the bathroom door; she looks pained when I open it. I can see that it's been one of those days when the client from hell has given her a roasting. She shakes her head as she looks at the mess; she's sweeping her eyes from side to side as though there are acres of destruction, when it isn't all that bad.

'I'll clear it up. Honestly Mum. I'll put it *all* back up. Just–' I'm about to say 'just leave it to me', but I don't bother. She already has: she's walked out.

I can hear her banging about in the kitchen, being too quick and energetic. She's also complaining loudly about her drive home: it was a nightmare, an absolute nightmare, especially in all this rain. Why, she's asking Ian, do there always seem to be twice as many cars about when it rains? Ian, who doesn't have a car, is saying 'don't ask me', but I'd have thought the answer was obvious. People want to keep their feet dry when it's raining, don't they? I keep quiet, though. It's not the moment to be a smart-arse, with the shower rail all bent and polyfilla stuck on the soap like a nasty rash. But I'll tell you something else: as soon as I get a car, I'll be driving *all* the time, whether it's raining or not. I'll live in my car.

Then I remember the girl. I pull off one sopping sock and actually get a better grip on the loo seat with bare toes, but I'm too late. She's gone. Nobody's around. There's nothing down there except headlights in the water as someone else turns into the estate.

'Frankie?'

I stick my tongue out and take a closer look in the mirror. The bite feels like an enormous gash. Actually it's only a small, dark dent in the tip.

'Frankie?'

I can see Lucy's reflection again but I don't turn round. My tongue is really sore. It makes you think about those blokes who have studs stuck through theirs. I feel odd even thinking about it. It must hurt so much.

'Frankie . . . '

Lucy's holding up the dustpan and brush.

'Shall I?' she offers. 'I could . . . if you like . . . '

I nod, sort of, and splash more water over my face. Lucy crouches down on hands and knees and begins to sweep up. She grins as I step over her.

'Poor *you*,' she says kindly. 'You didn't half go a crash. I thought you must have . . . '

But I don't listen. She never says anything interesting. I go out on to the balcony and lean right over so that any blood that's left pounds in my head and eyeballs. And I catch sight of her again. The police are down there now. There's a couple of squad cars with blue lights going but no sound and now I can see old Dave who always deals with trouble on the estate. He's talking into his radio and Liz Quiggley is by his side, talking into his face.

The girl in the skirt is standing apart. A young kid is beside her with his wild, scruffy head of dark curls pressed against the red folds. He's in boots: little green plastic boots, so he'll be all right in all this rain, even though he hasn't got a jacket on, just a jumper with a hole on the elbow. This kid is pressing his face against her legs, pushing, like he's trying to get her to move, only she doesn't. She's not taking any notice of him. She's looking up. I see her face slowly emerge as she scans the block of flats. It's as though she's looking for something special in that cold cliff face of stained concrete and dripping balcony rails. She's pale, very, very pale, and her hair is pale too, and outside it will soon be night. It smells like night.

A police van turns in next. It sends up a fan of muddy spray. Some people step back into their doorways. Liz Quiggley doesn't. She stays put with her hands on her hips. I can see the bulge of her white shins where her leggings end. She always has bare legs, even in winter. She's making a lot of noise down there. People are at their lace curtains now: they're twitching all over the place. This must be making Mrs Seagrove's day. Now I catch a glimpse of another group of people. They're strangers or foreigners, even, standing close together and not doing anything very much. I can even see their van and a glitter of glass on the ground where the windows have been knocked out.

Liz Quiggley steps forward but Dave is ready for her. He gets between her and the strangers and holds up his arms, like he's just about to dance away with old Liz. A little apart this girl continues to stare upwards until that curly-haired

11

kid, pushing now with all his strength, gets her off balance and she's forced to take a step. Then I notice that she has no shoes on, just flip-flops. Fancy wearing those in all this weather: it's tipping down. My sleeves are soaked and I feel chilly, but she's bare footed, almost. I can hear the rain drumming on the tops of the cars and see it streaking across the strengthening orange glow of the sodium street lights. Doesn't she feel the cold? Or is she used to it, being foreign? If that's what she is.

Then she staggers, stumbles nearly, and something swings free. At first I think it's ropes, or some daft thing like that, around her neck. It's clear that she's a bit odd, not to be wearing her shoes on a day like this, and in that skirt, so she could have ropes round her neck, couldn't she? Now I see that it's not rope, it's her hair. It's plaits. Her pale hair is plaited into two long tails that swing down way below her waist. I've never seen anything like this before, or only on telly or in books. So much hair . . .

She has lowered her gaze. Now she lets herself be herded back to the others by that little boy, like a lamb that nearly strayed away.

'Francis?' It's Mum again. Only her tone has softened. She knows she was over the top before because I didn't break the rail on purpose, did I?

'Help Lucy set the table,' she says quietly.

Suddenly I want to say 'no'. I want to turn round and yell 'No!' so loudly that Mum will leave me alone and that girl will look up again with her plaits swinging free. I want her to look up and see me.

No, no, no.

'It's soup first,' Mum says, 'so we need spoons too. It's

12

tomato, your favourite, Francis. Lucy, can you put out some bread? Or would you like toast?'

'I don't mind,' Lucy smiles. 'Bread's nice and toast. We like both, don't we Dad?'

But Ian isn't listening to his daughter. When I finally come back into the room, he's watching me and when I begin to plonk stuff on the table he gets up and goes into the kitchen to Mum. I catch them exchanging a look.

Mum draws the curtains across the window and smiles. They're new curtains, well, new from the charity shop, but still nice. She came home with them last week as excited as a kid, and I put them up. I'm much taller than she is, which isn't saying much because she's tiny, but it helps, she says, me being taller, at last. I don't really see why Ian couldn't have done it because he is taller still, except that he never does anything like that. He isn't interested, he says; it's *ideas* that get him going. But they're nice curtains, and just the right green.

'Mossy,' Mum said as she stroked them, 'and not too bright.' She couldn't think why anyone would want to get rid of them.

'Fashion,' said Ian, 'and style. I don't think green is really in any more. It's all minimalism.' He must have noticed her face fall, because straightaway he added that he, personally, hated that 'bleached' look in a house. It wasn't friendly. His sister's home was white and grey all over and always seemed cold, as cold as ice.

'Really?' Mum had asked him anxiously, looking back at all her green.

'Yup,' he'd grinned, and patted the sofa so that she went and sat down beside him, and he could be forgiven.

13

Now, as the soup steamed in the bowls on the table and the curtains swished across to shut out all the wet night, I suddenly feel guilty too.

'I forgot the tea,' I say.

'It's OK, Francis, I don't think we want tea, not with soup, do we?' Her voice is sharper.

'I do,' breathes Lucy, but so quietly that I pretend I haven't heard at all, even though I'm suddenly dying for a cup of tea.

I take a great gulp of soup instead and burn my mouth. My eyes are watering but everyone pretends not to notice. On my next, more cautious spoonful I actually taste the can. We've just done canning in chemistry: food cans are lined with different things depending on what's going in them, but the teacher said you can sometimes detect the metal, if you try. When I tell Mum about the taste she frowns and takes a slow spoonful. Then she shakes her head.

'Well,' she says, even more sharply, 'who's a clever boy today: because this, Francis, came out of a packet! And I can't taste anything wrong with it.'

'It's lovely,' says Lucy quickly, 'whatever it came out of. It's really nice. I *love* soup like this. It's so . . . toma-toey . . . '

Mum smiles at her, but I think she's pathetic.

I've got French, half a page of physics, and the rest of Act II of *Othello* for homework. *Othello*'s really complicated and I don't think I've got it yet, but it's fun, in a way, like a puzzle you've got to solve. As soon as Mum and Ian go out for a drink I make a start on it. Lucy's washing up. I did offer, but it's not my turn and she doesn't have proper homework. No one does in Year 7. Mum says that Lucy isn't doing very well at school and that Ian is worried about her. I suppose he would be, being a teacher. I wouldn't worry. She's just one of those girls who isn't interested. I've seen her sitting in class. She's always sitting by the radiator, gazing out of the window and half asleep.

Now I can hear her stacking the plates in the rack, letting the water drain away, washing out the sink. She's extremely . . . tidy. I'll give her that, tidy and clean. Soon she'll switch on the telly, but very quietly so that it doesn't disturb me. Mum always reminds her about that and I wish she wouldn't. When it's too noisy I can block the sound out. When it's low I find myself holding my breath, trying to catch what is being said. It's so annoying.

It's already dark outside, or as dark as you get in town. What I mean is: it's black outside my bedroom window and there are no stars at all. I never see stars here. Ian says that it's different in the country. In the *real* country, where he grew up, there were no street lights. He says that the nights are alive in the country. You can look up and see all the constellations in the night sky. He had a telescope, but he left it behind in the country, because he knew it wouldn't work properly in the town. His wife must still be there, in that house along a black country lane. The abandoned telescope will be in the attic, but I don't suppose she looks through it. He never talks about her. Nor does Lucy. They never say a word.

It's a good thing from Mum's point of view and only to be expected, I suppose. Like Mum says, Ian's 'considerate'. And so's Lucy, in a way. Sometimes, though, I wonder if I'm the only one who ever thinks about his wife, left alone in that house, along that dark country lane, with only the moon and the stars for light. Alicia. That's her name. Not Alice, Alicia; Alicia Bresslaw. When Mum learnt that she went really quiet. I don't think she'd ever heard the name Alicia before. But like I said, Ian never mentions his wife now.

'Frankie! Frankie, come quick!' That's Lucy. Or rather it isn't. It's so unlike Lucy to shout that I get up and go in, but she's only watching the box. She zaps up the sound and points open-mouthed at the screen. And I'm interested.

It's our block. It's us on TV. A wet news reporter, with her hair plastered down over her forehead and the rain lit up over her shoulder by the television lights, steps aside so that the camera can pick out the Council sign: Poet's Rise Estate.

I've never seen Lucy so excited. She's red in the face, and giggling. I snatch the remote control and put the sound up even louder.

'Police were called to the Poet's Rise Estate early this evening because of a disturbance. They have taken a large group of adults and children in for questioning. Local residents, angered by the floods of economic migrants from former Eastern European countries, say that these people, thought to be from the gypsy communities of the Czech Republic and Romania, are–'

'Look!' shrieks Lucy, leaping up and pointing. 'See?'

'What?' I'm playing it cool because I had noticed. It's only Mrs Seagrove's cat. It's creeping along the top of the wall behind the reporter. Then, at the wrong moment, it miaows loudly. The reporter has noticed too. She doesn't turn round, but her mouth trembles slightly, as if she's trying not to laugh. Then the camera cuts to a shot of the local police station.

'The gypsies are being held there and will be examined by a doctor as they are thought to have been travelling for several days, and may need medical attention.'

Or shoes . . .

'Dad and I saw them before,' explains Lucy. 'And Dad said there'd be trouble. Fancy them coming here. It's ever so exciting. I wish I'd been there, don't you Frankie? Then we'd have been on the telly too.'

'And?' I retort coolly.

She looks at me uncertainly.

'Then what?' I ask.

'Nothing. Nothing at all. I just thought–'

'You *don't* think, Lucy. That's your problem. You just say things.'

She nods, then smiles at me stiffly. That makes me even more annoyed. She always agrees.

'Well, if that's it then, I've got homework to do. It's pretty hard in Year 9. You've no idea how difficult it all is, especially Shakespeare. You have to work at it. But I don't suppose you've done Shakespeare yet, have you?'

'No,' she whispers. 'Not yet.'

3

·····································

Monday morning

Then I'm dreaming about her hair; at least I think that's what it is. She's undoing those plaits, untwisting them, and it's taking for ever. They keep twisting back up like yo-yo string, going round and round like . . . I don't know what. Then, absurdly, I'm dreaming about wood shavings and they are golden too, and coiled up. It's late afternoon and the sun is shining on my back through the school window, and I'm watching these coils roll off the lathe and drop silently down on to all the others on the floor of the CDT room. It's deep with them, like fallen leaves in a wood and suddenly I'm standing in them with my bare feet and the sun has nearly gone. I can smell them now. Sometimes, near the end of afternoon school, when the planks of pinewood have been fresh, you can smell the stickiness of the resin and touch it too, touch it, gently . . . And I'm touching her hair, almost, with my fingers.

And I'm awake. Suddenly, coldly, because the duvet has slipped off, I'm awake. It's too early even for a school day, which this isn't. This is Sunday and the gloom at my window means it's still night. I turn over and try to crawl into the leaves. I'm pressing my face into the pillow. I want to be back there again, even it it's only for a second, even a bit of a second. But it's all gone.

Mum is at my door. So it must be Monday after all, because yesterday was Sunday wasn't it? It was boring, raining Sunday. Now it's miserable Monday with PE first thing, which must be about the worst bit of time-tabling you can get. Not even people in teams want to do PE first thing on Monday morning. Barry will make us run, if he comes in. I just know it. He'll yawn redly, and rub his bloodshot eyes and look out of the window. When he sees the rain he'll decide to make us go for a run.

'Come *on* Francis!' he'll yell at me. 'Move it!'

I hate Barry but always do move it, in the end. Some of the other lads can make him back down. They're tougher than him, or just bigger. And they don't care: they feed him with weaklings like Sam and me. They offer us up like plump, pink shrimps tossed down in the path of a shark.

'That's right, you two,' they'll mock. 'Listen to what "sir" says and *move* it. Or some of it, if you can, Frankie.' Then they'll grin even more. They'll be lounging against the radiators in their grubby boxers, stroking their proper men's bodies, idly squeezing the vivid spots on their backs. They won't even bother pretending that they're going to leave the sour warmth of the changing rooms to splash through cold wet streets with the rest of us. They know what they're doing.

Actually, it might not be Barry today because it's Monday. It might be a supply teacher, one of those old ones who took early retirement but now come back to teach 'temporarily'. They're a complete pain. If it's one of them, he'll glance at

19

us eagerly, then check his watch again. He'll do a bit of running on the spot like he just can't wait to be off, as though at his age he's still keen. Some of these blokes are even older than Ian, but their sports stuff is always new. Brand new, often, and they're desperate to show it off. Stupid old gits.

At least Barry doesn't pretend to be keen. He hates PE as much as we do. The only difference is that he hates us more. And that's another thing I often think about: why is it that schools consistently manage to find these teachers who really hate kids? I've always wanted to ask someone that. I will one day. I'll ask Ian. One day, when he goes too far, I'll lean across the table, with Mum and Lucy watching from either side, and I'll ask: why is it that blokes who really *hate* kids, always end up teaching them? But I know what he'll do. He'll go quiet for a moment, like it's a serious point and he's considering it. Then he'll ask *me* what *I* think about it. I just hate that.

'Francis? Francis?' It's Mum again. 'For heaven's sake, Frankie, get up! We've overslept!' She's right: it's far too light outside and now I can hear the steady roar of the morning rush hour. This isn't Sunday. She's wet from her shower and as she reaches over to click on my bedside light, she drips on my homework. The ink runs on my *Othello* notes.

It's 8.21 already and now 8.22. How could we have both slept in ? The turquoise numbers flicker in the black clock like phosphorescence in a deep, deep sea. I must have hit the snooze button, then gone back to sleep. And her? She must have had a late night.

I don't remember my sports bag until registration. I'm

sitting there with my mouth tight shut because I haven't cleaned my teeth. I can feel that fur on them. I'm glad that it's only Sam at our table today. If it was Shelley and my breath stank, she'd have said 'pooh er!' and held her nose. Girls are so . . . oh, I don't know what. So talky. *All* the time. A bloke wouldn't mention it. He wouldn't say anything at all. But girls do. They say everything, especially if it's in front of a new teacher or a young one. They'll even talk about their periods. They say 'oh sir, *please* sir, I've just *got* to go, sir. It's an emergency! I've got my period. *Honestly*, sir!'

I lick around my back teeth, then blow into my hand and sniff, just in case. Actually, Sam looks as rough as me. Rougher, if that's possible. If he wasn't a mate I'd describe him as dirty. The teachers do, all the time. 'Quiggley,' they say sarcastically, 'don't you have any taps that work in Poet's Rise?' People say that when he was in primary, he always smelt of pee and had nits. You could see them in his hair. Walking about. None of the other kids wanted to sit beside him. They said their mums had told them not to. I didn't know him then. I don't really know him now. It's just that we live in the same block and often walk to school together. And sit together in registration. Sam Quiggley is such a quiet bloke that nobody knows him much.

It isn't Barry for PE. Once again he hasn't made it in. Mum always says she can't think how he keeps his job, because he's never in school on Mondays. People round here say that he has too much of a Sunday night of it and a Saturday as well, to stagger in to school first thing on Monday morning. Mum's threatening to complain about him to the school governors but I always ask her not to. It'd only cause a stink and my life wouldn't be worth living. And it's only games, after all. You don't need a GCSE in that.

The supply teacher is telling us to get changed. In the corner, away from the rest of us, Sam is undoing his shirt buttons very, very slowly. He's concentrating, biting his lip. I haven't said anything yet about not having my games kit. If it'd been Barry, I'd have told him by now. He'd have bawled me out but he wouldn't have done anything, not with Mum being a parent-governor and him not being himself on Mondays. That's Barry for you. He may be a bastard, but at least he's the bastard I know.

I don't know how to play it with this new guy. He's kind of marching about, watching us without trying to look. He's a little grey-haired chap with a tuft of moustache and a red face. Somebody mutters 'heil' and a snort runs through the room. He's heard it because he's suddenly studying his list very closely indeed.

'Right, lads?' His voice is too sharp.

'Right, sir!' That was someone from the radiator and I'll swear that one of them has raised his right arm in the fascist salute. The teacher goes redder; even the back of his neck is red.

Suddenly he jams the list into the pocket of his tracksuit. He flaps his arms at us, mutters something about stragglers and just sprints off. Some of the class follow. I suppose I would have, if I'd been kitted up, even though I can't run at all. Still, I'd have tried, at least until I was out of sight of school. Sam doesn't even bother. He buttons up his shirt and settles his scrap of tie back under his soiled collar. The rest of the class vanishes. As I leave the changing rooms I see Luke and Taylor watching the girls through the gym door.

Arshad is trying to, but isn't tall enough. The other two laugh and push him back down, patting his head as if he's a dumb Labrador pup or something. It must be a dance class in there. I can feel the floor shake as they crash around. Some of those girls are . . . huge.

I glance up and down the corridor. I could make for the library. It'll be warm up there and Mrs Morris won't say anything. She never does unless you mess with her books. Once, I said to her '*you* should have been a teacher,' but she just gave me a look and recrossed her legs. She must have been pretty, years ago, or elegant, which is what women used to be, isn't it?

I pause and look around for Sam but he's vanished too. Oh well. There's not much point in him being in the library when he can't really read. I might as well look at Act III. I like English. I like reading the parts in Shakespeare and I always volunteer, even though people groan, but someone's got to read them, haven't they – even though we've seen real actors do it on video. If it wasn't me, if I was someone else, who was thin, well, thinner anyway, I might have thought about being an actor.

In the library Mrs Morris is busy with little ones. Maybe it's Book Week. We did that in Year 7. She's pointing to a card in the catalogue drawer and they're gathered round listening.

'305.801,' she says. 'Now, who can find that for us?' A couple of little girls dash off straight away, all eager. Some of them are *so* small with their tiny, thin little legs in droopy black tights. I don't think I was ever as small as that. They're cute, though, these little kids in their new school clothes. Now she's handing out worksheets. That'll shut them up for a bit. It's all a waste of time, really. The library catalogue should have been computerized years ago, Ian says. I open *Othello* and begin to read. If Mrs Morris wanted help with the database, or stuff like that, I'd have given a hand. I'm good at that.

Then I notice the picture in the local newspaper. She's there. I almost don't believe it, but it's her, absolutely her. The black-and-white photo is grainy and I wouldn't have known it was her if I hadn't seen her, but now there's no doubt, even without the red of the skirt. She seems to have her hands behind her back. It must have been taken just after she picked that thing up from the puddle. She doesn't seem to want anybody to see what she's got. She's hiding something. But that's her skirt, her red, red skirt, trailing into the water. Only it's grey of course, in the newspaper.

'Ah. Francis. Just the man.' It's Mrs Morris. 'Have you got a minute?'

'Sure.' It couldn't be better. Now, if anyone asks where I was, I can say I was helping a teacher. It's almost the truth.

'I need,' she says, 'to lift this board up on to that shelf, there.' She's still struggling with it herself, which is daft, when she's already asked me. I bend close and smell her perfume again. It's . . . nice, actually. I think it must be the real thing: perfume, and not scent or the sprays that Mum has at home. They can be a bit much sometimes: they make me sneeze. It makes me wonder about Mrs Morris, using perfume like that, and in school, when she's so old. She's got grandchildren, actually, and her hair is almost white.

She insists on hanging on to a corner. It isn't that heavy so I whirl the board up smartly, to show her, and I put it firmly in place, only the heading, 'Current Affairs', is somehow upside-down. All her neat newspaper cuttings flutter off like autumn leaves. I feel a bit daft. I'd have got it right first time, if she hadn't tried to interfere. She only laughs and shrugs. Some of her grandchildren are about my age. She told me so. And she told me about their holiday together last year. It was Albania or Romania, or somewhere like that where tourists don't usually go.

It takes me ages to get the board sorted but in the end I manage to fix all the cuttings back under their right headings. The bell goes. I almost forget *Othello* but she runs after me and calls down the corridor. Without a word she takes the newspaper from my bag and puts *Othello* in its place. I feel bad because she's smiling. She thinks it was a mistake, as though someone like me would never nick the library newspaper on purpose. It's odd to think that she's a granny.

I haven't got a granny. Well, I *have*, obviously. What I mean is, I've never met her. She and Mum fell out years ago. I was the last straw, so to speak, not that there's much of a straw man about me! But I've still never seen her. I've never even seen a picture: Mum snipped her out of the photos after one row, so there's just my grandad with his pop eyes and her shoulder, in a checked dress, touching his. When I was little and other people's grannies used to meet them at the school gate I used to look out for one with a checked dress. I mean, she must have been a bit curious about me, mustn't she? I used to sort of pretend to myself that she was watching me from a distance and that one day she'd tap me on the shoulder and give me a present and say it was our secret and that I wasn't ever to tell June.

Sam gets free lunches so he often reappears at midday.

Sometimes he lets me have his puds. There isn't much point in him being in class anyway, especially not in something like English, because he still can't read, or not properly, and nobody ever asks him anything. He's just there, or not, like today. It never makes any difference, and all he does is doodle. Sometimes he fills whole pages with minute scribbly drawings.

'See that news thing on the telly?' I ask sitting down opposite him. 'That thing about Poet's Rise?'

He nods, shovelling in mashed potato and licking the gravy off his knife. He's splashed a bit on to his shirt.

'Your mum was–' I begin.

Lunch is meat pie with mash and beans. It looks quite nice. He stops chewing. His mouth is half open. His dark eyes are on mine.

'Your mum was so–' I was going to say something like 'wild' or 'far out'; but I hesitate. He's staring at me too much. He chews slowly, then swallows, like it's suddenly become painful or there's a bone in it. 'She was . . . pretty impressive . . . ' It's just the sort of shifty thing that Ian would have said.

'My mum–' he begins thickly. Then he drops his knife and fork down on to the metal tray. He gives the tray a shove so it skids across the table, smacks the salt over, then tips over my knees and down on to the floor.

'You . . . you don't know anything about my mum. So . . . you shut your mouth, you stupid slob!'

There's cheering all round. I grin but he doesn't. He kicks away his chair. A couple of girls nearby whistle through their fingers. 'Temper, temper!' they call. 'Don't get your knickers in a twist.'

26

Then, from nowhere at all, Lucy is at my elbow, dabbing at me with a tea towel.

'Lay *off*!' I yell, much too loudly. She backs away silently, sticking out her tongue to catch at a bit of hair. The older girls are dying. They're drumming their feet under the tables, flinging their arms around each other, sobbing with laughter. Last week there was a food fight in here, and people are keen. The pie is on my shoe as well as the floor. It looked fine when Sam was eating it. Now, spattered everywhere, it looks gross, like the sort of thing you see on pavements, after a good night out.

I go into the kitchens for the bucket and mop. One of the dinner ladies jokes that it wouldn't hurt me if I missed another lunch or two, would it?

I start to explain that it wasn't *my* lunch anyway: I didn't drop it! I'm only doing this for a . . . for someone I know . . .

She isn't even listening. She doesn't think much of me. I can tell. She thinks I'm a fat slob too. I take the mop but when I've cleared up the bell's already rung so it's too late to go back to the library.

When I get home I don't go straight up. I loiter in the car park. There's no one around, no one different. I do something that I haven't done for years and years: accidentally on purpose I drop a 10p coin into the puddle. Then I pretend that I can't see it. I must be quite good at acting because within a minute Mrs Seagrove is at her window.

'What you lost then?' She's opened it and pushed the lace outside.

'Nothing. Honestly.'

'What you doing then, standing there, getting your feet wet?'

'Nothing.'

'Don't you nothing me.'

'Honestly, Mrs Seagrove.'

'Do you think I was born yesterday?'

'Yes– no! I mean . . . '

'You're after my Snowy, aren't you?'

'Your . . . ?'

'Snowy! My Snowy. Now don't pretend you didn't hear me, because I know you did. I've seen you. You've been watching her.'

'Watching . . . ? Oh! You mean *Snowy*. Your *cat* Snowy.'

'Of course I mean my *cat*. I wouldn't call anyone else Snowy, now would I?'

'No.'

'And I know what boys like you do to cats. I've read all about it in the papers. *And* I've seen it on the TV. First you torture cats, then you attack old people. That's what they said. So I'm warning you, young man.'

'But I haven't even seen your cat. Really, Mrs Seagrove.'

'Liar! You was watching her the other night. I've seen you at it. I've seen you spying from up there, when you thought no one would notice. I've got my eye on you. All of you.' She is still muttering when she shuts the window. Silly old biddy.

The water has soaked through my shoes into my socks. I bend down to pick up the coin, because it is 10p, after all. Then I don't. I leave it, queen's head up, like she's drowned or like that other girl in Shakespeare, the one who lay down in the stream and drowned. I've seen special places like this where all these coins have been thrown into wishing wells or lucky ponds. They lie there on the blue tiles, beneath

28

heavy wire mesh, tossed in for luck or charity, as people make a wish.

I glance up as I make my wish. That's our flat, our balcony, up there. You can see it all so clearly from down here. When she looked up, that's what she would have seen. There's no doubt about it. And when she looked up, she'd have seen me too.

4

....

Tuesday 24 November

Mum is already at home. She's sprawled on the sofa watching *Neighbours* on her own. She hasn't done that for ages. I drop my school stuff by the front door and almost go and sit with her. Then I don't: I think she may have been waiting for me. She swings her feet off the coffee table and moves over to make room, but I refuse to notice. I go into my room and shut the door. I don't bang it. I only shut it. I sit down at my desk. I want to begin work straight away. Then I remember that my rucksack is out in the hall. I can't go past her again, not without saying something.

She's never home at this time. Not normally. I wonder if something awful has happened. Have they closed down the salon and made her redundant? You do hear of things like that, especially round here. One of those current affairs cuttings on Mrs Morris's board had been about redundancies at a big local garage. 'Thrown Out of Work 6 Weeks before Xmas': that had been the heading. One morning, when the mechanics turned up, the garage was still locked. The owner had gone bankrupt, so the twelve men, who'd worked there for years, had all lost their jobs. I'd read the article because I thought I recognized one of the men in the photo. They were lined up in their overalls in front of the locked doors. He looked a bit like the guy who's downstairs with Liz Quiggley. But I couldn't be sure.

There's not enough work for everyone round here. Some people blame the Channel Tunnel. They say it's taken passengers from the ferries. Other people say it's other things: that there are too many people looking for work. But Mum's salon wouldn't close, surely? People still seem to get their hair done. Even people like Mrs Seagrove, Mum says. And even if the salon did close, I know Mum could get another job. Easily.

Ian thinks she should anyway. He says that she could have a proper job, a 'career', if she wanted to. Mum always retorts that hairdressing *is* a proper job and that it's looked after us, hasn't it? Ian goes quiet then, because she's right. It has looked after us, her and me. She's always done stuff for me. I mean, she got me this desk and all the software ages before other people at school got theirs. The desk's a bit small now, but that doesn't matter. Not really. When I was a baby and she couldn't work in a salon she used to go round to people's houses, taking me with her. There's a photo of me in a little blue baby chair with curls and locks of hair dropped all round me on the floor. I don't think I can remember those days but sometimes, if I hear the close slice of sharp scissors cutting through thick hair, it can make me feel really odd: sort of excited but peaceful at the same time. It's a really . . . personal noise, isn't it . . . that noise of scissors, cutting through?

Actually, I suspect that Ian is embarrassed about going out with a hairdresser. His wife, that woman who's still waiting for him to return, was an artist. And still is, I suppose. She's down there waiting in the dark nights of the countryside. It's an artist's name, isn't it? Alicia. Alicia Bresslaw. A hairdresser called June isn't like an artist, not really, is she?

If I don't go to speak to Mum, she'll come in to me and I don't want that. I don't want her to knock on my door because I'll have to say 'come on'. She'll perch on the edge of my bed, determinedly not grumbling about the mess because she's got something more important on her mind. It'll be Ian. That's all she thinks about nowadays. It's 'Ian thinks this' and 'Ian believes that' all the time. I'm sure he's going to move in, only she won't put it like that. She'll ask me if I think it would be a good idea.

And what can you say to that? 'Yes!' 'No!' 'Don't give a damn–' maybe that's it! Maybe this time I just won't have an opinion. 'Do as you like, Mum,' I'll drawl, barely looking up because she always wants to discuss everything. That would throw her. 'Just suit yourself.'

Only she doesn't come in this time. She doesn't even knock on my door. She's running a bath. She can't be going out, not again. And Ian's away. She said he was taking his sixth form to some history conference in London. But she's carried the radio into the bathroom, which always indicates serious getting ready to go out preparations. Or maybe something did go wrong at work. This could be bath as relaxation.

I sneak out for my bag while she is safely submerged but am caught by the end of *Neighbours*. I'm still there, watching some cookery trash, when she emerges covered by a towel and a pale green face mask. She still doesn't say anything so I don't either, but I switch channels. The funny thing is that though I'm the teenager, Mum's the one with spots. It drives her up the wall. Poor old Mum. Not that she *is* old: I mean nowadays, thirty-one isn't old, is it?

'Oh, *there* it is. Pass my bag, luv.' She's mumbling through green lips and pointing to it in the corner of the sofa.

'About tea, Mum . . . '

'Tea?' She's genuinely surprised. A bit of face mask flakes off when her cheeks crack into a smile.

'You know? That meal we have in the evening. I thought–'

'Whatever you like, Frankie. There's something in the fridge, isn't there? Or soup? There's more of that soup you like somewhere. Have that, eh?'

'What about you?'

'Me? Oh – I'll get something after.'

'Fine.' But it isn't, and I don't ask 'after *what*?' I don't even ask when she comes back in dressed more smartly than I've seen her for ages.

She's even smarter than when she had to meet Ian's sister.

'Do you think it'll do?' she asks, smoothing down this straight, tight skirt. It's her funeral suit. I remember it now. She bought it for Grandad last year – well, for his funeral. Then she didn't wear it because she said he wasn't *that* sort of a man. I think she wore jeans, actually. I know I did, because I got looks from people.

'You look great. Honestly.'

'Not too . . . dull. Or too short?' she asks, turning round, smoothing it over her bum. But she's pleased with it. I can tell.

'No way. And "grey's the new black".'

'Is it?' She's smiling brightly, touching the carved black

beads that Ian gave her. They were his birthday present but she never wears them. Now they look just right and she looks so different. It's not just smarter. She's more serious, older actually, but I don't say that.

'Well,' she turns back at the door, 'wish me luck.'

'Good luck, Mum.' It must be something like a job interview and that's why she hasn't said.

'Thanks, luv. I'm going to need it.'

The lift must be out of order again. I can hear the tap, tap of her heeled shoes hurrying along the walk-way, then scuttling down the concrete steps. That's her all right. Despite her little legs she's always walked too fast for me. She's always dashed everywhere, trying to do everything.

At one time she went out several nights a week to a job in a pub, after the salon. She'd leave about eight, after I was in bed and return at midnight, or even later. It was a secret. I wasn't allowed to tell and I never did. She was afraid that if people knew I was alone they'd tell Social Services and get me taken into care. It was her greatest fear. And mine. I always imagined that Social Services would wrap me up in a blanket and carry me away. I saw that once on a black-and-white film. It scared me to death.

I'd listen to her locking the door behind her, then scramble out of bed and watch from the darkened window as she hurried out of the car park. She didn't drive then. Now I can see that it never was a real secret. Everybody in the flats must have seen her and known that I was on my own. And no one ever came with the blankets so I suppose nobody ever told.

I didn't mind being alone. Not really. And I'd almost forgotten about it until now. Now, watching her hurry off again, I suddenly remember how cold the glass used to feel against my forehead as I watched her disappear into the darkness of the night. It was so cold it hurt.

Tonight she isn't taking the car, so it can't be far. I watch her turn left on to the High Street. Then she disappears.

And so what? I don't care what she does. And I don't want tomato soup. It hasn't been anything special for years. I don't think it ever was; she just thinks it was. I open *Othello* but I'm hungry after all. I can't concentrate on it. There's nothing much in the fridge except yoghurts – they're for Lucy, Mum says, but I don't like fruit yoghurt anyway. The sliced bread is a bit mouldy. Normally I wouldn't mind because you can't see it once it's been toasted but after that dead pie at lunch, the green patches disgust me.

I want – chips. I take some money from the jar at the back of the cupboard and five minutes later I'm leaning on the counter, waiting for cod and double chips.

'Hi there!' It's a girl from school: a face I sort of know but without a name. Anyway she's older than me. She's tall and thin with glasses and brown hair pulled up into a ponytail so that her neck looks very long and white. Her fingers, rearranging the stuff on the counter, are long and thin too. 'I didn't know you lived around here,' she smiles.

'Yeah. In Poet's Rise.' I feel awkward because I still don't know who she is and when you tell people you live on the Poet's Rise Estate, they usually take a step back.

'Are you going to the meeting too?' She asks as though I should be.

'Well–'

'You can come with us if you like.'

'Well–'

'We're not quite sure where it is, so it'd be a real help. As you're local.'

'Fine.'

I know I should confess, admit that I don't know who she is or what this meeting's about, but I can't. The chip woman is rolling up my packet in splashed white paper and I realize that I haven't quite got enough. I shouldn't have had double chips. She looks at the money on the counter and frowns tiredly and begins to unroll the packet again.

'Here.' The tall girl holds out the other 30p.

'I can't.'

'Why not? It's only 30p!'

She makes me feel mean and just like a Poet's Rise kid, for whom 30p is a big deal. Suddenly I wish I wasn't going to any meeting. I want to slouch on home, watch crap on the box and wipe my greasy fingers down the side of the sofa.

She only wants chips. I should have guessed. People like her don't eat at chip shops, they just snack there, for fun. I could say that I've got to do something for a neighbour or that I've left the front door unlocked, but I'm afraid that she'd suss out the lie. She's chatting to the woman and doesn't seem stupid at all. So I can't escape. And how am I going to eat the fish? It's not like a few chips, not in a meeting.

The car waiting at the kerb is very large and very old: so old that a couple of lads are staring at it, but not like they're going to kick the windows in. They're staring in admiration. This girl smiles at them too and they back off straight away and when she opens the door I see that there are already several people inside.

'Get in then.' She gives me a shove and then another on

my backside too, even though she has this posh way of speaking.

And it's too late, or too soon, or something awful anyway, because I can't sit down. I can't get into the minute space they've opened up for me. If I try, I'll end up half sitting on one of them. I *know* that's what'll happen because it's happened before in buses and things. Now I *never* try to squeeze in.

She must understand because she wriggles into the space herself and says 'thanks' to me, like I've held off on purpose to let her sit there. Then someone nudges me down into the well of the car amongst their shoes and feet. I put my hand out to steady myself and touch the back of the seat. It's leather, old, sleek leather, and as soft as skin.

'OK then?' The driver turns the key in the ignition. The car whines and wheezes but nothing happens. 'Blast it.' She tries again and in that moment when nobody is speaking and we're all willing the car to start I smell something. Down there crouched amongst these legs, I smell something, something I recognize even through the fish and chips. It's that perfume. It's Mrs Morris's perfume. I can't turn round to see but I know who the driver is. Then I recognize this girl. She's the granddaughter, the one who went on that holiday. She's Katy and her sharp knees are jabbing into my ear as though she couldn't care less.

It takes time to find the place where the meeting is because I don't know either and then it takes ages to park. In the end we're quite late. There's only standing room at the back of a church hall. Mrs Morris, who had said 'hi Frankie' as though she wasn't at all surprised to see me, makes her way down the centre gangway to the only empty seats right at the front. She doesn't seem to realize that the guy on the platform stops speaking and that everybody is turning to look at her. She even waves to a few of them. Now she's beckoning us. A couple of people from the car follow her. One's still eating chips.

'Come on,' she says quite loudly, as though this is fun.

I hang back. I mean, I want to know what this is all about. It could be anything, even religion, except that I'm sure I've seen Liz Quiggley and a couple of her older boys over by the exit. Mr Rashid from the newsagents is in the middle. No way am I being made to sit in the front. This isn't school. I'm staying put.

This girl, Katy, hesitates, then stays with me.

'At least,' she says, 'we can make a quick getaway.'

More people pile in. It's quite hot. She's so close that the end of her ponytail tickles my ear. The guy on the platform, who's in a suit, is rabbiting on about housing or something. I'm not listening. It's too hot and I'm worried that people can smell the fish. I can't hear him properly anyway. It's a bit like assembly at school. There, people sort of shift around because it's never interesting. Some people even nod off, or pretend to and some of the hard lads will snore. I can't see why all these people have come and I'm thinking how amazing it is that this girl is Mrs Morris' grand-daughter, when out of the blue, Liz Quiggley yells:

''Ere! Put a sock in it! Let someone else 'ave a go!'

There's a row then, with some people trying to hush her up and others saying, 'Go on Liz. Go for it!' I still can't make out what it's all about but Liz Quiggley is doing OK and she knows it. She steps aside from her sons and tells everyone to 'shut the f— up'. And they do.

Then, from some place in that hall, Mum begins to speak. Her sharp little voice is as brittle as a breaking nail on a blackboard. It catches me in the pit of my stomach, and for a moment I think I'm going to throw up.

5

....

Tuesday evening

The hall is falling silent, not suddenly, but row by row, like ripples widening around a stone dropped into a pond. And Mum is at the centre of it. I'm shocked. I'm struck and stuck, like I've fallen on to the rotten, rusting spikes of an old black railing. Her voice tears right through me. I'm too choked to concentrate on what she's saying. I can't even follow the individual words though they are as clear and sharp as a string of glass beads fallen on to mud. Then I catch sight of her. She looks really small amongst so many people packed in row by row in their bulky winter clothes.

They're listening to her, turning their necks this way and that above scarves and hoods and shabby fake fur collars. They're nodding in agreement. Even Liz Quiggley nods. Liz refolds her arms and tucks one leg up, balancing against the wall like an old, fat ostrich. Then she nods again at Mum even though they are old enemies. And do you know what I'm thinking? I'm thinking: 'Christ! If only Ian was here now! He'd be listening to *her* for a change! That'd give the stuck-up git second thoughts about hairdressers.'

Applause almost swamps her but she doesn't give up. One

of the Quiggley boys is leading it, clapping his hands noisily above his head. Then he scratches his stomach, hitches up his jeans and opens his mouth.

''Ere! Let's have a bit of 'ush again. For the lady!'

Mum smiles her thanks nervously. Liz is watching Mum like she's grown two heads. Mum carries on. She's talking about housing or something and waiting lists. She knows about stuff like that because we were in bed-and-breakfast for ages one year. It was no fun at all. The audience are listening. They understand what it means. I can't think why Katy and her grandmother are here, though. People like that are never in bed-and-breakfast. They always have their own homes.

Mum's voice is steadier, quieter: she's talking about . . . history really, about 'English tradition'. I suppose she's learnt that from Ian. Then, from the back of the hall and quite near me somebody says: 'that's racism, that is!' Mum must have heard although everyone instantly boos and jostles the guy who spoke up. She turns right round to face the challenge.

'No!' she says, her voice tense and cracking again. 'No! This *isn't* racism. And I'm *not* a racist. I've lived and worked around here nearly all my life, so this is my *home*. I'm from Poet's Rise and proud of it. Nobody can call me a racist because I'm *not*. And I can prove it: I get all sorts in my shop, black, white, pink, yellow – you know what I mean – and they wouldn't come, would they, if I was a racist? Eh? No! This isn't about race, it's about . . . space!'

A murmur runs round the hall. People are repeating what she's just said: 'this isn't about race, it's about space'. They're smiling at each other. You can tell that they approve. Mum grips the back of the chair and goes for it again. 'This isn't about race, it's about *space*. There isn't enough space for us all. That's the truth and I'm not afraid to say it! Not like some people.' She flashes a look towards the back of the hall. 'That's why I'm not afraid to say we can't have no gypsies *here*, especially not these Romanian gypsies, or wherever it is they come from. They shouldn't be allowed in, especially not into Poet's Rise! I say: send them back!'

'Oh God,' groans Katy into my ear. 'What a nasty, stupid, ignorant little woman!'

I don't say a thing. Not a single word. I just hug the fish and chips tighter and know that I want to escape, or die, whichever is quicker. I don't want anyone to see me either, especially not Liz Quiggley and her boys. Or Mum. Or Mrs Morris. In fact, I don't want to see anyone, ever again. I hate stuff like this. I can't imagine why they made me come to this stupid meeting. Why can't people just leave me alone?

'I'd like to say something–' Mrs Morris has stood up amongst the snarling, muttering crowd. 'Please–' she begins. Her thin hands are clasped in front of her as if she's worried about something. You can see her amazing large ring. 'Please . . . all of you . . . we can't agree with the view . . . ' she's barely raising her voice but this isn't school and nobody is listening. I don't either. I don't want to hear what I know she'll say.

I make for the exit. I'm pushing my way out, shoving past, actually, and treading on people's feet. I jostle roughly against the shoulders of an old man and I don't care. At last, I'm outside and quite alone. It's dark: it's a cool, orange night with cars and people passing by on the wet night roads and they're all too busy to notice me. And that's good. That's what I like about towns: all these people leaving each other alone.

Suddenly, I'm ravenously hungry. I tear open the paper. The cod's cold. The chips are even colder and all squished together because I've been holding the bag so tightly. I don't care. Not in the least. I stuff so much into my mouth I can barely chew. I can feel the fat on my tongue, smell it on the tips of my fingers.

Anyway, why should people like Mrs Morris, who doesn't even live around here, come and interfere? I don't go over to her street and tell her what to do! She should mind her own business. I'm disappointed actually. I always thought that librarians were a bit different from teachers but they're not. They're just the same boring little nobodies who get off on bossing kids around. It's like the army. They're all power crazy too. I break off a chunk of fish and crunch it up, silver skin and all.

'Frankie!' I recognize Lucy's voice immediately. 'Frankie! Over here, Frankie!' I don't really look up but I can't avoid her. She's at the bus stop outside the Red Lion with her mates Kelly and Moira. She's smiling so widely I hope her face splits.

'Frankie–' Moira and Kelly have changed but Lucy still has her school uniform on. After a whole day in it she looks as clean and neat as a child in an ad. She's smiling like one too. I can't avoid them so I chew violently and swallow it down.

'Hi Frankie!' It's the hundredth time she's said it. Lucy is *so* dumb.

'What's up?'

'Nothing.' She giggles. 'Nothing at all.' She glances down

at her hideous new shoes which are like clumps of black motor tyres. Kelly snorts and pulls at her top.

'So? Why'd you call me over?' I want Lucy to feel really stupid in front of her friends. 'What's happened *now*, Lucy?'

'Nothing. And I *didn't* call . . . I just . . . '

'Just what?' I demand although I know what's happened. When she saw me she must have nudged her friends and blurted out: 'Look! That's Frankie Johnson! My dad's going out with his mum!' Then the friends shrieked: 'Never! Not *your* dad and *his* mum! That's disgusting!' They fell about refusing to believe her so she protested. Then they'd dared her to call me over. She'd been dead keen until they started to inspect me and to snigger between themselves. Girls like Kelly and Moira only go for the lads. The worse they are the more girls like them. Everybody knows that. People like me and Sam, well, we *never* get a look in, do we?

Lucy is still staring at her shoes. I'm stuffing chips into my mouth. I don't care what they think: couple of slags like that! My lips sting with the salt. I should walk away, but I don't. I can't think where to go because they're staring at me so much. They're checking everything. They look me up and down, as slowly as tigers, and then they look at each other and grin. There isn't any sign of the bus. The four of us are stranded there on the damp pavement and I can't walk past because as soon as I've gone, they'll laugh even more. They'll laugh out loud and it's not fair. I can't help it if I look a bit big from the back. I know what'll happen if I walk on. I know what these girls are like . . .

And then I see her again. She's coming up the High Street, towards me.

'Look at *that*.' Moira tugs Lucy's sleeve. 'That's one of

44

them, isn't it? One of them gypsies that's flooding in?' They crowd together, suddenly silent. If they really were tigers, they'd have been crouching down now, ready to pounce.

She's alone. She's walking very slowly, not looking at anyone but gazing up at the buildings as if she's sleepwalking – not that I've ever seen anyone sleepwalking, apart from on the telly. At the Red Lion she stops, bang in the middle of the pavement so that a couple walking behind nearly bump into her. She's so close I can see where her hair is pulled too tight and is crooked. If it was unplaited, and washed –

'You looking for something?' demands Kelly.

The girl doesn't move. She doesn't even turn round. She tilts her head back and looks up at the roof of the Red Lion. She's examining it as though she knew it and was looking for something special up there. I can see her eyes darting to and fro. She's moving her hands too. It's as if there might be music somewhere: as if she can hear it and is marking out the rhythm, but I can't hear anything at all.

Kelly opens her mouth to yell, but doesn't. She wrinkles up her nose and shrugs and sucks her thumb instead.

'Silly cow,' she sniffs.

'My dad knew some real gypsies,' says Moira shyly. 'On the fairgrounds they were. He says they're all illigiterate: you know, haven't been to school so they can't read and stuff. Or write. He says that they make thumbprints instead, but that they're not . . . bad people. It's just that they're stupid, not being able to read. And it's a shame, he says, because some of them are all right, when you get to know them.'

45

The girl is feeling in the pocket of her long red velvet skirt. Now she is taking something out.

'My dad–' Lucy begins excitedly.

'Yea?' drawls Kelly. 'What about your dad? Honestly, Lucy, your dad is *such a dish*. So go on then. Tell us. Do you know, I could fancy your dad, Lucy, if he wasn't your dad, that is!' They're all giggling hotly together. Then they whisper loudly, their heads touching. 'Your dad's so . . . ' Kelly squeals and glances back at me. She scans me from head to foot, slowly and deliberately, then licks her lips. 'He's *so* attractive. Anyway I like *older* men. If you know what I mean. My sister says that older men treat you right! And she should know because her bloke's twenty-five!'

'Twenty-five–' They're screeching and laughing and falling about. 'So go on, Lucy. Tell us what your gorgeous dad says.'

Lucy takes a great, gasping breath. Then she sticks out her tongue and captures an end of hair and chews. I can hear it crunch between her neat white teeth.

'He says–'

'Look!' I interrupt. 'Isn't that the bus?'

'So what?' says Kelly. 'Haven't you seen one before?'

I don't care. At least it shut Lucy up. I don't want to hear about Ian Bresslaw. And I especially don't want to know what he thinks about gypsies. I don't want to hear anybody talking about gypsies ever again.

When I turn round the girl has disappeared. The pavement's empty. Surely she can't have gone into the Red Lion? Not her. Not on her own. Passengers are spilling off the bus. One of them is Mr Rashid, so the meeting must have ended. Any minute now all those people who heard what my mum said could be coming along this pavement too.

I can hear the girls shrieking and stamping their way to the upper deck. It's those shoes that they all wear, those dumb shoes with heels like hooves. They tap at me from the window and squash their noses and lips up against the steamy glass but I don't wave or anything. They are so sad. They are even sadder than Liz Quiggley.

As soon as the bus moves off I run the length of the High Street. I run back. She's not here, nor in the side roads. I'm positive but, just in case, I cross over and jog up the other side. I'm panting when I get back, but I haven't found a trace. She's vanished. If the girls hadn't seen her too I might have wondered if I hadn't imagined the whole thing. I don't even know why I want to see her again. I mean, with those people from the meeting coming along, maybe it's a good thing she's scarpered: out of harm's way, and all that. I should go too, but I don't. I can't, actually.

6

....

Later

An alley runs alongside the pub. I don't know where it leads because I've never been down it until now. Tonight it's dark and narrow and wet with ivy or something else dark and shadowy, hanging off the fence. It seems to be full of things left behind: piled up against the fence and then just left. It's the only place she could have gone. I squeeze past a barrel at the entrance and my heart thumps high up, in my throat and ears. It's because of the running. I'm not very fit at the moment.

There's a wheelie bin on the right. It's stuffed with rubbish: pub rubbish, I should think, and it smells horrible. There's more underfoot. I've squished something that may not be rubbish at all, but it's too narrow and too dark in here so I don't bend down and look. I take another couple of steps. I'm feeling my way along the sodden, softened fence. Rain from the ivy flicks on to my cheek and neck. It's quieter in here, away from the road: too quiet, maybe. When I stub my toe on the corner of a crate the bottles jangle so suddenly and loudly that it startles me. And as that sound slips into the night I hear something else. Somewhere, just in front of me, something has moved. Someone is in the alley with me.

'Hello . . . ?' My voice sounds pretty feeble but I try again: 'Hello?'

It's so still. It's like being wrapped round in wet black velvet. I hold my breath, trying to hear her breathe. My ears ring.

Suppose it's someone shooting up? Or a couple, maybe, in the dark. Or . . . anything, really. It could easily be some drunk or homeless guy settled in amongst the rubbish, because that's what it's like around here. You just never know, especially in the dark. Things happen round here in forgotten places like this. Doesn't she realize that?

'Hello there . . . ' She'll understand English, won't she? Everyone understands 'hello' nowadays.

'Hello . . . ?'

No one replies. Only the rain trickles into a gutter and behind me music from the juke box suddenly rolls against the warm red window of the pub. If I don't make a sound I'll find her in the end. She can't hide forever, can she? I take a few more steps. It's narrower here. I can't see the road at all now, only the blur of headlights as the cars pass by the entrance. I can smell rotten wood and rust and thick black city mud. And something else, that I almost recognize.

If she's in here, she might be close enough to touch. I move my hands slowly in front of me and touch . . . nothing at all.

'I'm . . . I'm . . . ' I stammer. Then stop. I can't do it. I can't explain or take another step . . . or anything at all. The wet black cloth of night is being wrung too tight. I want to get back into the light. I'm . . . a coward. That's how I

49

should be introducing myself. That's what I am. I'm a hopeless, stupid idiot. A fat git. A slob. A mummy's boy, a teacher's pet, and cheap too. That's what I felt in the chip shop. A lard arse, a wanker, but above all, a pathetic coward. I'm someone who is afraid to go on. I want to, but I can't. I just can't. I can sort of imagine finding her, touching her hair, which would be wet now, in this rain. I can imagine it, but that's all. If I wasn't afraid, I could do it, couldn't I? I could do everything, then.

Step by step I edge backwards, groping my way and stumbling as if I am the loser who has been sleeping it off amongst the rubbish. Outside again, in the rush and glow of the street, I feel better. It was just that alley being so dark. Mum's always said that you should stay away from places like that. It's commonsense, isn't it? I mean, what's the point?

I perch on the bit of wall outside the Red Lion and realize too late that it's soaking wet. Still, it doesn't matter. Nobody can see when I'm sitting down. And I'm going to wait around because I'm still convinced that I'm right. Someone is in the alley.

Ages ago, when we were in bed-and-breakfast places, Mum saw a mouse. I can remember it really clearly. Our room had one of those very small television sets bolted on to a metal shelf on the wall. She and I had to watch it with our heads bent back because it was too high up. One evening while we were waiting Mum screamed and jumped up on top of the bed. She tried to haul me up too but I wouldn't because you couldn't see the screen at all from the bed and it was that thing about firemen which I used to love.

Anyway, I can remember it so clearly because Mum never does daft stuff like scream, but she did that time and boy, could she scream! It frightened the life out of me so I began to howl too and people came out of their rooms and banged on our door to ask what was up. 'It's a mouse,' Mum wailed, 'or a rat. And as big as that!' She was balancing on the pillows in her stockinged feet holding her hands miles apart. Someone got the landlord and he got his shovel and I remember thinking how dumb that was: no mouse was going to sit around and let itself be shovelled up. I didn't realize that he planned to bash it over the head. Somebody brought a bit of mouldy cheese and someone else produced a mousetrap, but Mum wouldn't get off the bed. Not for anything.

After a bit everyone got fed up and wandered off. The landlord began to say that she must have imagined it because he'd looked everywhere, and anyway, there hadn't been any mice around recently. Mum still wouldn't get off the bed, though she did eventually sit down with her feet well tucked up. Hours later, when everything was quiet and everybody had gone back behind their shut doors, and I'd fallen asleep where I was, huddled up in my clothes on the little sofa, Mum said she finally saw the mouse come out from behind a cardboard box. It crept slowly across the floor and its thick black tail slithered behind it. She saw its bright eyes and when it picked up the crumb of cheese, its tiny, pinkish paws were just like a doll's hands. She watched it sit back on its haunches and nibble away and she didn't move a muscle, couldn't, she said, even if she'd wanted to.

When the mouse had finished the cheese, it cleaned its whiskers. Then it made its way across the bit of carpet, over the flex from the electric fire and then, without a backward glance, it slithered out under our door. And she just watched. The landlord didn't believe her. I think there was a row because she complained to the housing people and we left soon afterwards. Still, she'd been right. It was a mouse. She'd seen it in the end.

Mum can be very . . . well, pig-headed. Sometimes. And sometimes, though not often, I wish I smoked. Like now. It'd be useful because then I wouldn't just be hanging about on a wet wall. I'd be doing something and people would recognize that. I wouldn't be addicted to it and unable to stop. I'd just be someone who smokes now and again. Like Ian really. But I'm not going to smoke. It's such a disgusting habit. Look at Liz Quiggley, or my grandad. Mum says he smoked himself to death. You should have heard him coughing in the morning. He coughed like other people stir mud. It was disgusting. If I heard him during breakfast I couldn't eat a thing. I used to imagine that brown, bloody stuff churning around and bubbling in his chest. It made me want to throw up because sometimes he spat into the basin and didn't wash it away. So I shan't ever smoke. I don't want to be like that. He smelt too. He smelt like old people smell and though I was fond of the old boy – after all, he was the only grandparent I'll ever get – nevertheless, I never particularly wanted to hug him or sit on his knee like you're supposed to with grandparents. I hated his lank, smoky hair and his thick orange fingernails. When I was really little I didn't realize that the colour was tobacco dye. I thought that Grandad must be picking wax out of his ears with his fingers! I bet Ian Quiggley will be like that when he's an old man. I wonder if Mum's thought about that.

Still, I could do with a quick drag now. I have had a puff or two because Sam smokes roll-ups, but I haven't smoked a proper cigarette from end to end. Sam's ciggies always come unstuck and moult bits of tobacco on to your tongue and that's gross, but I could spit them out and people wouldn't think 'what's that guy on that wall up to?' They'd know: I'd be a bloke smoking a fag.

I'll just have to be a bloke eating fish and chips instead. At least I've still got them, even if starting on them is a bit like reopening a grave. The chips are definitely dead. Still, who's to know, in the dark?

I'm acting out this scene that they're still hot and crunchy, just in case somebody is watching me, when something in the alley moves again. There's no doubt. I can hear it. There it is: a definite rustling. It's a sound I almost know, this rough, squeaking rustle. It isn't paper. No: it's polythene bags. It's part of supermarket noise: the rustle of the bags at the checkout, as people fight to get them open. Of course.

So she *is* in there. Poor thing. She must have been hiding at the very far end holding bags of groceries or something, and too frightened to move. I feel awful because it was me she was frightened of, when I'm the last person in the world to do her harm. It's odd that I hadn't noticed her carrying anything – but that must be because she'd hidden the stuff down there earlier. That would be it. Now she's come back for them.

I don't know much about gypsies, apart from films and the things people say, but I think that's the sort of thing that gypsies do, isn't it? They have to hide things because they're always travelling. They bend sticks over and make signs with leaves to mark their routes. They also hide stuff for each other behind hedges in country lanes. That was in a book I read. Here, of course, there aren't any hedges, so she had to do something else. Poor thing. It can't be much fun, and in the rain.

I shift up a bit, so it doesn't look as though I'm lying in wait, and the last bit of fish tumbles off my lap.

'Miaow!'

'Ow!' I scream – well, it wasn't a real scream. It was more a yelp, but it must have been loud because a woman at the bus stop turns and looks at me. I scowl. Silly cow. I couldn't help it.

This cat shot straight out of the alley, sprang at my knees and then leapt off. It was the smell of the fish, I suppose. Anybody would have yelled if a cat had attacked them like that. It was quite out of the blue – or out of the black, in this case. Like lightning.

Then I recognize it: it's Mrs Seagrove's lost cat, Snowy. Bloody stupid name. It's mewing around my feet now, sniffing the edges of the paper, rubbing its head against my shin. It's a long-haired cat and it always looks a bit tatty. There's rubbish and stuff caught in its tail. If the woman at the bus stop wasn't still watching, I'd kick the brute back into the alley. It really startled me. And it's too fat. I flick over the last chip and it mews more. The woman smiles at me before turning away, but I still scowl. I can't see any joke.

I pick Snowy up gingerly. There's no point in waiting here now. She purrs thickly. She's very warm, considering the rain, and she's quiet as well – quiet as a mouse, actually, until I turn in to Poet's Rise. Then she starts to struggle. Doesn't she like the estate either? I slip my hand under her collar but she's twisting this way and that and I'm afraid she'll get away. I'm not going to let her after getting so far. Her claws slash through my anorak but I don't mind. It just makes me even madder. Stupid, ungrateful, vicious cat. I don't care if she scratches me to ribbons. I'm not going to let her go now, the ungrateful beast.

' 'Ere!' Mrs Seagrove appears from nowhere. 'How dare you! What do you think you're doing with my cat!'

'I'm . . . '

'I'll tell the police about you! And the animal protection people. I'll have you persecuted!'

'I *found* her, Mrs Seagrove. I've *brought* her home! For you–'

'Don't you lie to me as well. I know a thief when I see one and you've got thief's eyes, you have. You've been planning to steal my Snowy for weeks, you nasty little boy!'

What can you say? Snowy settles instantly into Mrs Seagrove's arms. The old woman leans over her talking gently; she strokes her head and the cat rubs its muddy paws against her wrinkled old cheeks.

'Did he take you away from Mummy? Did he?'

'I *didn't*! She was down the alley by the Red Lion.'

'There! I always knew you were up to no good! What were you doing in the Red Lion at your age? I shall tell your mother about you.'

'Go on then!'

But when she raises her old, worn face to look at me I see that there are tears in her eyes. They're trickling down her cheek and on to Snowy. I open her front door for her and she goes in still muttering, with the cat cradled in her arms like a baby.

Now there's no escape for me. The raised scratches on my hands sting horribly. I have to go home now. I might get blood poisoning. I can't put it off any longer. The light's on in our flat. Mum must be back. I'll just have to go in and face her, in her sharp black suit with Ian's black beads round her neck.

7

....

Saturday morning

'Oh!' Liz Quiggley is standing outside our front door on Saturday morning. 'It's you–' she's acting surprised. Did she expect someone else to be living in our flat? She picks the fag off her lip and holds it down behind her thigh, like she's a little bit embarrassed about it. Her emptied mouth bends up into a wet pink smile. I'm shocked. I don't know what to do. She's never smiled at me before; laughed at me, maybe, and yelled, most definitely, but smiled? Never! Smiling is not Liz Quiggley's style. I don't smile back. I gawp at her thick red neck. She's got a small moustache. She doesn't know what to do either, so here we are, on Saturday morning, either side of the door and too close for comfort.

'Oh. Is your . . . is June in?'

'Yes.' If it was anyone else I'd have already stepped aside and called Mum, but it's different with Liz.

She's never been inside our flat. Mum's always said these awful things about the Quiggleys. Everybody does, round here, but it's usually in secret. After all, a couple of years ago old Liz was in court for fighting! She'd beaten up this other woman who was supposed to be seeing Liz's bloke. She wasn't sent to prison, but she was bound over, Mum says, whatever that means. Looking at her now, and she's spread right across our doorway, it's hard to imagine anyone binding old Liz up, or down, or any way at all. People are scared of Liz Quiggley and her sons. With the exception of Sam. Like I said, Sam's such a nonentity that he doesn't count at all. He couldn't scare a fly.

Mum comes out of the kitchen with a tea towel and a plate still in her hand.

'I was thinking,' says Liz quickly, shifting her weight to the other leg and knocking down a trail of ash, 'about those things you said, June. And that letter . . . with the names. That letter against the gyppos.'

Mum rubs at the plate. Liz takes a quick, deep drag as though her brain needs it. I can see Mum looking a bit anxious. Normally I'd leave her to it; now, however, I stand beside her. The hall is so narrow our shoulders are touching.

'About that letter–' Liz goes for it again. Mum glances at me with a 'get lost' look. I refuse to recognise it.

'What letter?' I ask.

'Yes?' Mum is ignoring me. Totally. It's obvious that she knows something I don't.

'I could help with that. Couldn't I? What do you say?' Liz asks.

Mum is rubbing that plate to death.

'I know everyone round here,' Liz continues, 'and what's more,' she begins to laugh, 'they know *me*! Don't they? Eh?' Now she's roaring. She's herself again and shrieking and shaking with laughter as if she's the funniest thing on earth. Mum is thinking on her feet. She's good at that and usually quick enough to head off trouble. You have to be, in hairdressing: she always says that few things make people as wild as a bad hairdo. People's hair matters a lot. So sometimes you have to think really fast. Now she looks up and her brow unwrinkles. She must have decided how to get rid of Liz, which she needs to do before Ian turns up. Liz and Ian . . . would not be good together.

'Francis,' Mum says, 'could you just watch the toast for me?'

'Toast?' I can't believe it. She's getting rid of *me*! She might as well have told me to go and play in my room. She wants to speak to Liz Quiggley on her own.

Well. If that's what she wants, that's what she can have. Toast indeed! If she really *is* making toast, I hope it burns. I hope it burns as black as soot. I hope the whole flat burns down, then the block, then the Estate. I hope that when I come back, *if* I come back, then Poet's Rise is just a smouldering ruin. Only it won't be like that, will it? I've seen those places on television, where they've had wars and bombs and massive explosions with scuds or patriots or whatever those smart missiles are called. Even then blocks like ours never burn away to nothing after the explosions. They're left standing along the streets like stumps of rotten teeth in a dead man's jaw. Even after everybody's been killed, or buried, or just gone away, even then the concrete is still there, and the ugly, jutting balconies.

In the car park I pause for breath. I look up at our flat. Had she shared my thoughts when she stood here with her skirt in the water and stared up at our block? Had she seen how ugly it all is? I bet she had. I bet she's come from some little mountain village where spring comes suddenly after the snow melts and lambs and little goats leap from rock to rock. I've seen these places on the telly. There are golden stooks of corn in steep summer fields and the farmers use horses and carts. Secretly, she'll be missing her homeland. I mean, who wouldn't? And who would want to come *here*? I wouldn't. Not if I could choose.

They were talking about this in school yesterday – well, arguing, actually. I didn't join in. I don't know anything about this and, like I told them, I'm not even interested. It's nothing to do with me, is it, if Mum has such a thing about these gypsies, or whatever they are? This girl, Vicky Jackson, said that these people who call themselves refugees are actually parasites and scroungers, who just want to come to England and live here free. It's because of our welfare state, she said. When Ahmet asked her how she knew that, she said her father had told her. Anyway, she added, the newspapers had written the same, and she should know because she does a delivery round before breakfast, and she always reads the headlines! People sniggered because it was a dumb thing to say. Then they looked at me, because after that meeting everybody seemed to be talking about 'space not race'. It's supposed to be a sort of campaign, but I'm not involved. No way. It's Mum's thing. So I shrugged and said 'don't look at me' and went on eating my lunch. Vicky Jackson snorted: 'don't flatter yourself big boy, nobody *wants* to look at you – it's just hard *not* to!' Then everybody laughed.

I took no notice. It's the only way. Still, I could have told them a thing or two. I could have said: 'Hey, who are you kidding? Do you think a girl like that would want to end up in a dump like this? I bet her parents made her come here. I bet they push her around just like your parents do. This is all

60

their idea. She'd have been much happier staying in Romania, or Czecho – whatever, in some little village in the mountains, even if there isn't any electricity or running water.' Anybody who'd seen her in the car park could have seen how unhappy she was. Why else would she have been staring at those blocks? She thought they were prisons, not homes!

That's what I could have told Vicky Jackson and her friends, only I didn't. It was too much trouble. And they wouldn't have understood because they hadn't seen what I'd seen. Anyway, recently, and especially since that public meeting, everything seems too much trouble to me. It was much better when there was just Mum and me living our lives. We both knew where we were then. Now –

''Ere!' Mrs Seagrove has scuttled out of her house. She's wearing a flowery nightie with a pink thing on top. She's not a pretty sight. ''Ere!' She must have been lying in wait for me, spying on me from behind her curtains. 'I've got something for you,' she spits. She hasn't put her teeth in yet.

'Got something?' I hesitate. I'm not keen. No way. Knowing Mrs Seagrove, it's likely to be a good slap round the ears.

'So you'd better come in. And mind you wipe your feet. I can't have you messing up my carpet.'

There doesn't seem any escape, so I follow her. At least it's better than being at home.

The heat hits me first, then the smell. It's that charity shop stink of old winter coats and cardboard suitcases and odd, unmatched cups from the houses of dead people. It reminds me of my grandad too. He always wore the same knobbly brown jumper, summer and winter, morning or evening. I think he slept in it as well.

Mrs Seagrove leads the way into her sitting room where an electric bar fire glows like an angry red pimple in the gloom. I don't even want to be here. There are too many other things bundled all over the sofa, but I perch on the edge, amongst them. She has disappeared. There is an old, greasy pillow beside me with her hairs on it. That's it, of course. This little room is where she sleeps and lives. This is all of it. In winter it's hard enough for us to keep our flat warm. Ian says it's the damp and the thin walls, but at least we get a bit of sun. Down here, on the ground floor, where they put the old folk, there's no sun at all, so it's freezing. There's no view either. It's like a cell. No wonder she's always twitching her curtain aside. And I bet she only has her pension. So this is it, for her and Snowy. ''Ere you are then.' She's holding something out to me: a small bar of toffee.

'Thanks . . . thanks a lot, Mrs Seagrove . . . but . . . ?'

She draws the pink knitted thing around her. I suppose it's a shawl, or was, because now there are great looping holes. She's scowling an anxious, gummy scowl, while her dentures grin quietly at each other in a jam jar on the telly.

'I jush' may,' she spits, 'have been a bit hashty. About . . . Shnowy, that ish.' She sits down on a squeaky cane chair opposite and pops her teeth in. 'It was Peg what told me: my friend Peg Warburton, that is. Your mum knows her because she goes to her for a perm at Easter. Anyway, she told me. Sometimes she sees my Snowy down the High Street. Quite often, she said. So it wasn't you that took her. Not really. I can see that now. It was the food.'

'The food?'

'From the Red Lion. That's where Peg sees her. They throw out the food – perfectly good food too, Peg says, because her daughter works there. A wicked waste, Peg says, but at least the cats get some benefit. And my Snowy's a regular.' She gives Snowy a proud glance. 'There's bits of steak and shrimps and half chickens with chips, and all sorts, because folk are ever so fussy nowadays. Nothing's good enough for them, is it? It's not as if I don't feed Snowy proper, because I do, but–' she gets up and shuffles around, straightening a thing or two. I can see the blue veins wound round her skinny legs like thick ivy stems on an old, bent tree. My grandad was like that too, only it was on his hands and wrists. 'Ink blood' I used to call it, because his veins reminded me of the cartridges you put in pens. Sometimes I can picture him so clearly that I can't really think of him as 'dead', even though he's the only person I've known who's died. Mum didn't even cry. She just wore her jeans and held my wrist very tight, like I might run off.

'I thought you'd like the toffee,' says Mrs Seagrove, adjusting her teeth again. 'You do, don't you?'

'Ye–es. Definitely. Thanks a lot. But you shouldn't have bothered. Honestly. I only brought Snowy back because you said. She'd probably have come on her own, wouldn't she?'

'I daresay. But you can't help worrying, can you, with all the traffic? And the dreadful things that you hear about. Because people do terrible things to cats, don't they? It was on the telly the other night. Terrible things, like it's fun.' She shakes her head in a puzzled way.

I nod. I've seen that programme about cruelty to pets too and I've read about it because Lucy's keen on animals and has those magazines and things. She'd like to be a vegetarian, but Ian says she mustn't, not yet. Some of the pictures in her magazines are really disgusting. I feel uncomfortable looking.

'You can try a bit, if you like,' says Mrs Seagrove.

'Try a bit?'

'The toffee, lad. I used to love a bit when I was a girl. I can't now. Not with these teeth. It gums them up and I'm afraid they'll snap. But don't let that stop you. Go on. A big lad like you needs to keep his strength up.'

She watches keenly as I peel off a corner of cellophane and try to sink my teeth in. It's too hard. I might as well have tried to bite the handle off a saucepan. My jaw's aching but she's laughing, so I wonder if she knew about this before.

' 'Ere!' She snatches it back from me as if I was a toddler. 'This is how you do it!' She crows triumphantly and smashes the block against the edge of the window-ledge. It shatters and she laughs again and for a second, I glimpse the cheerful girl she must have been. Mum talks about this because lots of her customers are OAPs. Sometimes, when a hairdo's gone really well, these old dears smile at themselves in the mirror and Mum says it's as if they're seeing the reflection of how they once were, years ago, when their hair was thick and shiny, and rolled up in plump curls, just like the film stars. It makes the job worthwhile, she says.

'My dad used to make toffee for us,' Mrs Seagrove continues, 'when we were nippers. In a great big iron saucepan, it was, over the fire and you could smell the butter and the brown sugar. Lovely it was, though our mum said it tasted of smoke.'

64

Her voice has gone soft.

'This is . . . lovely too. Honestly, Mrs Seagrove.' I've managed to free a chip of it and it's beginning to dissolve.

'That was the only *nice* thing my dad ever did for us,' she carries on, not listening to me at all. 'He'd buy the ingredients himself, the sugar and the butter and . . . and almonds, was it? I forget, you know, but he'd do it over the open fire with us kids watching, and then pour it out, very quick, on a couple of big plates. For a treat it was'

'You had . . . a real fire . . . in the house? For cooking? I can't imagine it.'

'Not in the *house*, in the *fields*, this was, when we come out to do the hops. That's when our dad made the toffee. I suppose he had a bit extra in his pocket, because we were all working. The whole family picked hops. Even little children did as soon as they could reach the bins. It was strawberries first, then raspberries, and hops was later. But that's when he made the toffee. That was in the hop fields.'

'How do you mean, "you came out"?'

'Out of the East End! I wasn't *born* in Kent. Not *here*. I'm a Londoner, really. We come out each year for the hops. Everybody did in our street.'

She's looking round the close, dark room as though suddenly she doesn't think much of it. And I don't blame her.

'Yes,' she sighs, and ruffles up Snowy's huge belly of tangled fluff, 'but they were happy enough days in the hop fields. Especially for us children. With all that . . . air.'

'Didn't gypsies go hop-picking too?'

She doesn't answer, just pulls that pink thing tight across.

'I thought . . . I mean, I read somewhere, that gypsies did

65

that too: you know, picked hops, and fruit and lavender. And made clothes pegs. And–'

'I wouldn't know about that,' she says, her voice suddenly harsh. ''Ere. Just look at that time! I can't have you hanging about under my feet all day and me not even dressed!'

Outside again I don't even glance up at our flat. Let them get on with it. I hope Liz Quiggley's driving Mum crazy. I hope Ian comes round early and Liz just stays on, talking and talking and talking, and dropping ash all over the carpet. It would serve Mum right. I don't want to go home now. The trouble is, there's nowhere else.

8

....

Monday 30 November

I don't believe in horoscopes or star signs. Mum does, I
think, and Lucy too. So do people at school. They're
always reading them out but I'm not interested. I overhear
them, obviously, but I don't *believe* that stuff. It's all
coincidence, isn't it? If some 'expert' writes: 'you may
experience financial problems when Saturn is in its final
quarter', they're on to pretty safe ground, aren't they?
Especially round here. So when this magazine mentioned
'unexpected changes and a stranger who will come into
your life around the twenty-ninth or thirtieth of Novem-
ber', I didn't believe it. I just read it. I wouldn't have even
done that if it hadn't been Sunday, the twenty-ninth, and
a really rotten day as well. And if Monday hadn't been the
thirtieth . . .

The odd thing is, today is almost the first time ever that
I've been pleased to get up and go to school. I do all right in
school, well, more than 'all right', if I'm honest, but I don't
like it. There are too many people milling around; but I
know I've got to stick it out. Anyway, even though today's
Monday with Barry for PE, I didn't mind because I have this

feeling. It's probably because of the weekend. Mum and Ian must have had some sort of row because he wasn't there when I finally went back on Saturday. I knew he'd been: he'd left his *Guardian* in the hall and Lucy had come too. I could smell her. I always can. It's this scent that she sprays on: it makes my nose itch. Well, they'd come and gone. Mum hardly mentioned my absence. She made this really special supper which wasn't for them. It was for us, though she didn't say so. I didn't ask but I was quite sure. She had that look about her. After we'd eaten she sat hunched up on the sofa and we watched *Blind Date* which we haven't done for ages. Ian always groans and rustles his newspaper about if it's on, and that spoils it.

I thought: here we go again. She's had these bust-ups before and it gets her down, even when the bloke has been a total loser, like Brian. Brian was *so* bad. You hear about kids running away from stepfathers like him – not that he ever was my stepfather – but I'd have run away, if I could. I didn't because there wasn't anywhere to run. Luckily they had this almighty bust-up over money, *her* money, or as she said later 'our' money. He'd been nicking it. And other stuff: daft stuff like our hammer and a blanket, as well as the radio. He said he'd only borrowed it but we knew better. It's like an illness on this estate. Everybody's nicking things. Anyway, I was really pleased to see Brian go even though Mum was dead miserable. We saw him later in the supermarket with a baby in a buggy and an over-loaded trolley. He was crashing into people and being a total prat. I told Mum we'd had a lucky escape.

Mum doesn't want any more children, thank goodness. If anyone ever mentions it she always says: 'What? At *my* age!

You must be joking!' and they usually are. Anyway, she's too old now, isn't she?

She'd been crying though, in the night and on Sunday morning she shut herself away to do her accounts. All day. She can't be disturbed when she's doing accounts so I had to answer the phone. All these people were ringing up about this petition to keep the gypsies or travellers or whatever they are out of the estate. Some of the callers were OK but some were really rude. After a bit I told them she wasn't in, but they kept on ringing. I got so fed up I left the phone slightly off the hook and escaped with a pile of magazines into the bathroom. That's when I read this horoscope. There wasn't anything else left so I ran in more hot water and browsed through that rubbish.

It made me feel odd. It's like the lottery, isn't it? You don't believe you'll ever win, yet always, watching those balls tumble around, you can't help . . . hoping. In that second or two before the wrong numbers line up, your brain races like mad and you see exactly what you'd do if you did win. It's like dreaming when you're awake. Well, that's how I felt when I read that stuff about this stranger coming on the twenty-ninth or thirtieth. Hopeful and excited at the same time.

I still feel like it this morning, even though it's school and Barry made us run again. I didn't mind. It wasn't raining and I thought I might see her, or that little curly-haired kid at least. They might be . . . walking about, mightn't they? Then we could smile. She could drop something as I was jogging past and I could pick it up and she'd say 'thank you' in a little foreign voice and her plaits would swing forward.

But they weren't around. I'm glad, in a way. Running

makes me so hot. I go red in the face. My legs go red too and that is actually worse, that and sweating so much. I'm still sweating in English so I move to a cooler seat. Sam, who never goes red, stays slumped against the radiator as usual. He always looks cold: cold and clammy.

We're doing *Othello* again, and it's that bit where Iago gets Cassio drunk. Afterwards Cassio says something about drink transforming men into beasts. We're just discussing that when this happens.

Someone knocks. The door opens and it's her. Unbelievably. She's hanging back behind a couple of other people and the deputy head, Miss Chester. Our English teacher, Mrs Rushmore, looks up from *Othello*. Ted Stoppard, who's reading Iago today, trickles away into silence. We're all staring at the girl. We've all gone quiet. The teachers go into one of those huddles in the corridor outside and mutter. She's left out of it. She's standing on her own, by the board, staring back at us – or not quite. She's looking over our heads as though the ceiling and its cracks and corners are more interesting. I can see her eyes darting about. I follow her gaze, but there's nothing up there. Only cobwebs and some brown stains where the labs above flooded last summer. I suppose she's nervous. After all, it must be pretty scary, mustn't it, to start school in another country? I wouldn't like to do it. No way. And that must be why she's here: she must be coming to our school.

She isn't wearing that skirt, thank goodness. Straightaway I lean over and look at her feet, but it's OK. She has some shoes; not black ones, like you're supposed to for school but a pair of bright red trainers. The girls will soon put her right about that. And the socks. None of them wear socks like

70

that: up to the knee and patterned. Not even the really little girls. As we all watch, she reaches out and touches the board. She draws a straight line, looks at the tip of chalk dust on her finger and almost smiles.

Somebody in the class titters. I don't suppose they meant it unkindly and to be honest, she does look . . . different, but Chester has heard. She leaps back into the room. An angry frown is chiselled into her forehead. She scans us, row by row, and we all lower our gaze. Her nickname is the Axe, partly because her first name is Alexandra, but you can see why it's stuck. She's brutal. Even the lads give her a wide berth.

'Haven't you got something better to look at?' she snarls. We all nod and look back at the play, except Sam. He scratches his ribs and settles more comfortably against the radiator. Now he doodles swiftly and lethally all round the text. There wouldn't be much point in him looking at the words. He doesn't understand.

So maybe that's why the Axe does it. She pushes a bit of her rough red hair back behind her ears and points to the empty seat beside Sam Quiggley. My seat.

'There you are,' she says, jabbing in its direction. She steps aside to give this girl a better view of the chair. We're all holding our breath. All watching. The girl doesn't move.

'Yasmina?' whispers our teacher. 'Could you . . . maybe . . . '

And Yasmina does. She gets behind the girl and steers her towards the empty seat then sort of pushes her down a little bit. She is sitting on the very edge of the chair, with her legs stuck out awkwardly in those odd, patterned socks. Sam never stops doodling.

71

Then the Axe says her bit about us looking after our new 'visitor' and helping her in every possible way. We are to make her feel welcome. Her eyes seem to linger on me as she speaks and I'm quite pleased. She can trust me to help. I expect she's heard about me in the staffroom. People know I look out for Sam and Mrs Morris has probably told Miss Chester about all the time I spend in the library.

'Now,' says Mrs Rushmore, when the others have gone, 'back to work, eh? Sam? Will you share your book with Emilia?'

'Emilia!' Vicky bursts out. 'What? Like in *Othello*? The woman who's married to the villain – what's his name? Iago, isn't it? Honestly, Miss? Is it really the same name?'

'Yes.' Mrs Rushmore reads from the piece of paper which the Axe had brought. 'Emilia Radu.' She smiles at the girl who doesn't smile back. Then she writes the name up on the board.

'What a coincidence,' says Yasmina. We're all chattering and staring and flipping through the text to find the name of Iago's wife and be sure.

Emilia doesn't know this, obviously. She isn't doing anything at all. She's still perched on the edge of her chair and keeps glancing sideways at the window as though she would fly through it if she could. I can see her hands, her fingers nervously pleating and unpleating the stuff of her skirt. Everybody's stealing a quick look at her. It's such a coincidence. However nobody except me really knows what a huge coincidence this all is: that she's here, almost beside me and sitting in *my* place, with her thin yellow plaits of hair snaking down her back, and over *my* chair. And it's the thirtieth.

'Right,' says Mrs Rushmore. 'Settle down, shall we? Cassio? Iago? Ready? Ahmet! I *said* settle down.'

Ahmet grins and finds the place because he's Cassio today, but I can't even see the lines. I don't think I'll ever settle down again. The words aren't clear at all. If I could, I'd reach across and touch her hair. That's all. But I shan't. I know that you can't do that sort of thing.

Once or twice I look across at Sam. He turns the pages for her, when everybody else does, but I know it's only pretend. He always pretends. Actually, I think the Axe has done a really dumb thing, making her sit there. She'll never learn from Sam. Nobody could. She should be with a girl, Yasmina, for instance, or Marie; those two are all right and sensible. They'd look after her properly. Or me. I'd do it. I know about looking after people. I'd make sure she doesn't get lost or miss lunch or –

'Francis?'

I look up, startled.

'Aren't you with us today?' Mrs Rushmore has crept up on me. She slaps her hand flat on my book, then turns it slowly around. Now it's the right way up. 'There,' she says with grinding sarcasm. 'Is that better?'

'Yes,' I mumble. 'Thanks.'

Her look is not friendly at all. The whole class laughs at me. Surely it wasn't that funny. They're roaring like idiots at absolutely nothing at all, yelping with laughter as though they've been dying to do this all morning. It's awful, and what's even worse is that this girl, Emilia, might think that they're laughing at her. It's so dumb it hurts.

I look over quickly. She's almost smiling too, as if some-where here she knows there might be a joke after all. I look at her face. I can't help it. And she's like . . . well actually I can't say what she's like. But I can see *something* in her face, something happening, and it's the most . . . beautiful thing I've ever seen. It's . . . different. As I watch, Sam pushes back his fringe of hair and scratches under it. He glances at her, just for a moment, and gives this almost smile too. He's just a copycat; as if either of them can understand what's going on . . .

Mrs Rushmore is flapping her arms about. Iago's voice quivers. He's going to crack up. The whole class is seething. Does she imagine her flapping will dampen down the frenzy that's crackling like fire? The bell rings. Everybody's jumping up, ramming their chairs under the tables, yelling about lunch or clubs or homework. Or just yelling. They thunder past Mrs Rushmore who has given up flapping. Yasmina's fighting her way against the tide.

'Come? Emilia?' She's holding out her hand, encouraging her, like you would a child. 'Come. You. Come? Yes?'

I'm cramming my books into my bag because I need to go with them.

'Francis.' Mrs Rushmore puts out her hand.

'Francis–'

A group of girls is leaving the room in a gaggle. Emilia and Yasmina are somewhere in the middle. Shelly's there too. I can hear her squawking.

'Francis.' Mrs Rushmore has caught hold of my arm. 'Just a moment, please. I don't quite know how to say this, but, you won't forget will you, Francis, that whatever happens at home – whatever's said *there* . . . it's different in school. I . . . we . . . we like to think that *everyone's* welcome here. In our school.'

74

'Yes. Sure.' I smile back. It's my serious obliging smile, but I'm keen to go.

She should be telling that to a loud-mouth like Vicky! More likely: she wants *me* to spread the message around. That's obviously it.

I hurry out but I can't see them. I run to the end of the corridor and tear down the steps but they're not around. It is so unfair and shortsighted of the teachers. That gang of girls will scare Emilia to death. Breaktime is a nightmare, especially if you're new. She'll hate it. She might be so put off that she never comes back. And then I'd lose her again.

Sometimes I just don't understand teachers at all. Fancy making a girl like that sit by Liz Quiggley's son! It's asking for trouble, as Mum would say. Positively sitting up and begging for it.

9

....

Tuesday 8 December

'You should see her hair, Mum.' I follow her into the sitting room. 'It must be down to her knees. At least. It's amazing and so . . . so fair.' I've been trying not to go on about Emilia, but this just slipped out. 'You'd *love* her hair, honestly. All the girls at school do.' One or two have even plaited their own hair into wispy tufts that stick out and flap when they run. Emilia has made quite an impression in school.

Mum frowns. She doesn't *love* anything at the moment. In fact she looks seriously sad. Yesterday Ian turned up. He hasn't been round for over a week. He told me he'd had a lot of marking. He needed to catch up. He told Mum that they needed to talk. I took the hint and went out, even though it was really cold.

I walked up and down the High Street twice. Then I looked in all the windows. I could have gone running, couldn't I, if I'd thought of it and if there hadn't been so many people around. It made me think. Running would be something to do when I've nowhere else to go. And you get to see stuff, don't you? It would feel quite different if nobody was making me run. I could train in secret and I'd get so good that one day I would effortlessly power past everyone else to cross the finishing line miles ahead. I might even do a marathon. That'd throw old Barry. I'd get a cup or a medal and up there, on the rostrum, I'd give that victory salute. I'd be so fit I wouldn't even be out of breath. Or red.

I might lose a bit of weight too or 'fine down' as Mum once put it – but that isn't the reason I'm thinking of running. I'm not in the least bothered about being 'cuddly'. Lots of women think it's really attractive. There's 'more of a man to love'. I read that in one of Lucy's magazines.

On my way back yesterday, I came face to face with Ian on a bend in the stairwell. I could see at once that things were better between him and Mum: better but not perfect was my guess. At least he was running down lightly, not stamping or shuffling. He wanted to talk. I could see that too.

'Look, Frankie–' he began.

'What?'

'About this . . . this gypsy thing–'

'You mean Mum's campaign?'

'Yes. Except that it's not really your mother's campaign, is it?'

'Isn't it?'

'No. No it isn't. But that's not the point. The point is what do *you* think about it? Francis?

'I dunno.' I saw irritation pucker his face.

'What's your mum playing at? I mean, she's never been interested in politics before – has she? Why's she doing this?'

I looked him up and down. Suddenly I liked him even less. So that was it. He might pretend that a little hairdresser wasn't quite his type, but secretly it suited him fine. He liked her that way. He didn't want Mum to have opinions of her own. He was putting her down. He didn't want her to talk about things that were important to her. He was jealous. He wanted her to shut up. I bet that's why he broke up with his wife, with that Alicia. He couldn't deal with her being an artist while he's just a boring old history teacher. I bet he didn't just leave. I bet she *threw* him out.

'Don't you have *any* ideas, Francis?' His tone was sarcastic.

I still didn't answer. That made him boil. It does with teachers. You don't have to be rude or pull faces to get them frothing at the mouth. You just have to keep quiet but look them in the eye so that they know you're holding out on them. It always works. So at least I've learnt something from the lads.

'June's playing with fire, Francis. She really is. I don't think she understands . . . I mean, life's really tough around here. You and I know that, but your Mum–'

'You don't think Mum understands that?' I said it very slowly and sort of looked around, which isn't easy in a concrete stairwell, but I wanted him to realize how dumb he was.

'I don't mean it like that, Francis. I meant . . . Oh forget it!'

He passed me but now his step was hard and heavy. The two-faced git. He wouldn't have talked like that to Mum. He'd have been all affectionate, especially if I wasn't around. He'd never have dared ask her 'what are you playing at?' If he had, she'd have been mad now, not sad. She'd have kicked him out and opened a beer for herself and a coke for me and said 'good riddance to bad rubbish', even if she didn't mean it.

By the evening he still hasn't called. Her tea is on the kitchen table almost untouched. She hasn't eaten a thing. She hasn't even put on the telly.

'I don't think,' I begin again, 'that Emilia's hair has even been cut. That's like Sikhs, isn't it? Those men don't cut their hair, do they? Ever.'

She looks up now. I'm happy. I've caught her attention.

'Shut up Frankie!'

I do.

'Can't you shut up about that wretched girl, just for a *minute*?'

'I only said–'

'*Shut up!*'

I do because she's screaming. She's red-faced and bug-eyed and suddenly I don't like her either. She's been seeing too much of Liz Quiggley.

'I'm going out,' she croaks finally.

'Good." I say it under my breath so that only my lips move. But she knows.

It's so peaceful in the flat after she's gone. It's too early for telly so I get *Othello* and stretch out with him on the sofa. I'm not going to wash up. If she wants to flounce out, fine. But I'm not clearing up after her, especially when she hasn't touched her fish fingers. She's just smeared them with tomato sauce. Normally I'd perk them up in the microwave and scoff the lot, but I don't fancy them now. They disgust me.

She's still not back at nine. Then Lucy rings.

'Hi Frankie!' Her voice is so bright. 'It's *me*!'

'I know. What's up?'

'Nothing.'

I wait. I can hear her at the other end, breathing noisily. I'm cool.

'Is . . . is my dad there?'

'No.'

'Oh.' I hear her disappointment, but I don't care. She's not my problem, except that suddenly she's crying, sobbing into the phone, barely able to get the words out. She expected Ian back *hours* ago. She's scared. It's nearly ten.

'Have you seen him, Frankie?' she whispers, between sniffs.

'Sure. He was round here earlier.' I'm casual: casual and cheerful.

'Was he?'

'Well, I think it was him. Very tall guy with brown hair?'

She tries to laugh but I can hear her swallowing down tears.

'Is anything the matter, Lucy?' I let my voice register a little surprise, as if I've only just noticed something's up.

'No. Nothing. Honestly Frankie. I just wondered. That's all.'

'OK then. If you're *sure*. Bye.'

I can't believe I did that. I wash up now and tip Mum's food into the bin. It'll be eleven soon.

Out on the balcony it's so cold that I wonder about frost. There aren't many people around. It's not the night to be out. They must be together someplace: my mum and her dad. They must be sorting something out because nobody could quarrel for six hours. Eventually she'll lay her head on his chest. She'll 'paddle with the palm of his hand', just like Iago said. I've seen them do it.

There are a few lights still on in our blocks. One is burning in Mrs Seagrove's flat. I'm surprised. I'd have expected an old woman like that to go to bed early. I mean, what's she got to stay up for? Nobody's going to call at this hour. It must be pretty cold in that room of hers. She should have drawn the curtains. It would have helped.

Halfway down to the car park I go back up for the fish fingers. They'll be my excuse. I'll say that I was putting the rubbish out when I thought of Snowy. She'll appreciate that. Old people do. They never waste food. My grandad used to joke as he cut the mould off bread: he called it his penicillin sandwich. While I'm down there handing over the fish fingers I can keep a lookout for Mum's car. Just in case.

Mrs Seagrove's front door is wide open now. The bare bulb in the hall is too bright. My heart pounds. I wish I hadn't come down here. Life *is* tough round here. Things happen and I don't need Mr Knowall Bresslaw to tell me.

'Mrs Seagrove?'

Last month kids followed this old guy into his flat; they tied him up, then helped themselves to the shopping he'd just brought in. They threw some of it at him. Ice cream and stuff.

'Allo luv.'

I gulp. She's not dead. She's carrying a bucket and mop. Snowy purrs between her feet.

'I just thought I'd do a spot of cleaning,' she says cheerfully. 'It's such a nice, bright day.'

'But–' Then I notice that it's a full moon. She's dragging the mop over the step but the dirt is smearing, not shifting. Can't she see that? It's so cold that it might actually be freezing.

81

'I've brought something for Snowy.'

'Have you?'

'Fish fingers. If she's allowed to.' I open the bag. Snowy stretches up against my leg. She mews, then scratches.

'Well! I must say this is a surprise. Did your mum send you?'

'No. She's . . . out. I think.' I put the fish fingers on the wet step and Snowy pounces. She doesn't mind ketchup at all.

'I don't suppose you've seen my mum?'

'No. I can't say I have, luv. Gone, has she?'

We're standing side by side in the cold white light. Around us the quiet blocks lean up into the sky. I don't want to go home. I don't want to climb the empty stairwell, to turn my key in the lock, to close the door behind me. I don't like the dark.

'About your mum.'

'Yes?'

'I *did* see her, now I think about it. I can't think how it slipped my mind. It was much earlier on and we spoke.' She gives me a sharp look. 'I wondered if that was why your mum sent the fish: to say sorry.'

'Sorry?'

'Well. We didn't just speak. We had words. And I'm afraid I had to speak my mind. About those gypsies.'

'The gypsies?'

'That's right. These folk from abroad that they want to put on the estate. I had to tell your mum what I think. I may be an old woman but I still know what's right and I'm going to say so.

'I'm sure Mum'll be really pleased. She needs everybody's

support.' I speak stiffly. I'm freezing and I'm tired of people involving *me* when they should be speaking to Mum.

'Support?' Mrs Seagrove throws the mop into the bucket so roughly that water splashes up. 'Support! So *that's* why you've come, eh? Now she's sent you to buy me off, eh? Support? You thought a bag of your leftovers would change my mind about the gypsies? Well, you're wrong, you cheeky bugger. All of you. Now get out before I call the police.'

I retreat.

'I'd never have let my Snowy eat that fish if I'd known it was a bribe. You've probably poisoned it, you and that mother of yours!' She grabs the mop again and waves it at me. Dirt flicks off on to my face. She's mad. And I back off.

'We haven't poisoned it. Anyway, it's nothing to do with my mother. She's not even here, is she? She's gone: I don't know where she is and I don't care. *I* brought that fish for you, Mrs Seagrove. *Me.* I thought you'd be pleased. It was for Snowy. And I don't know what you mean about a bribe. It's only fish fingers.'

She's drawing her cardigan around herself and rubbing her hands.

'Well,' she mutters more calmly, 'it's getting late, isn't it?' She looks about her nervously as if she's only just noticed it's the middle of the night. She won't look at me, just at Snowy.

'About the gypsies, Mrs Seagrove . . . ' I don't know what I want to say; it's just that I want to talk. She scoops Snowy from the step. From the safety of Mrs Seagrove's arms the cat gives me a jealous yellow glare.

A night wind gusts around the corner of the block and in

the gutter an empty can scratches to and fro. It's bitterly cold.

Somewhere out there Emilia will be asleep. The covers will be pulled right up and her long plaits will be coiled warmly around her shoulders and back.

'I can come tomorrow, Mrs Seagrove . . . '

'Why? Why should you come tomorrow? Got too many scraps, have you.' But she hasn't slammed the door.

'No. It's not that: it's about the gypsies. I want to talk about the gypsies.'

'I don't know anything about no gypsies.'

'*Please*. Mrs Seagrove.'

'Well. I'm busy tomorrow, very busy, what with Snowy and–'

'I could come after school. About four? Like . . . for tea?' She stares at me, then turns and goes back into her flat, but she doesn't say no.

10

....

Wednesday

'Frankie! Over here, Frankie!' Lucy is with her friends at the school gate. I wave, sort of, because I don't want to be late. Today I'm going for tea with Mrs Seagrove. Lucy runs over.

'Wait for me, Frankie. I've got something for you.'

'What?'

'It's nothing special. Honestly, I don't suppose you'll like it anyway. It's only–'

'Go *on!*' Her friends are urging, giggling. 'Go *on*, Lucy. Show him!'

'What is it?' I don't want to be interested but I am. Lucy pulls a book from her school bag. Her straight, blunt hair swings like a wing across her face.

'Not *that*, Lucy,' Kelly protests. 'Don't be such a wimp! Show him the *other*. Oh go on, Lucy, *please*.'

'No!' Lucy blushes. 'Shut up, Kelly. I don't want to!'

Is she going to cry?

'Here.' She shoves the book at me. 'Take it.'

'Wow. Thanks.' I'm a bit underwhelmed actually. It looks like some tatty old copy of Shakespeare. 'What's it for,

Lucy?' She really is dumb. Why should I want two copies of Shakespeare?

'You said it was difficult to understand,' she's gabbling breathlessly. 'When I told Mum, she said you could have this. She doesn't need it any more. She–' Lucy stops suddenly. She never mentions her mother normally.

'Oh Lu–cy,' the girls groan, 'you're hopeless. Honestly.'

People are pouring out of school. A wave of them pushes us apart.

'If you don't want it . . . ' Lucy mutters dully. I'm about to hand it back. At that moment Emilia comes out with Yasmina and Sam and some others. I stare. She's still wearing her red shoes. Everyone's told her not to but she doesn't seem to understand. Or care. Today she even has red socks: red and ribbed with a stripe under the knee. I think they're football socks, actually.

'Sam! Wait for me!' I yell, only he doesn't. He waves and doesn't wait. He's walking between the two girls. He's so close, their shoulders are touching. Liz would have a fit if she knew. An absolute fit.

Somehow, in that crowd and turning round to watch Emilia, I drop the book. It isn't exactly my fault because Lucy could have held it more securely, couldn't she? It's face down in the mud and someone steps on it.

'It doesn't matter,' Lucy says quickly. 'It doesn't matter at all. Honestly Frankie, it's nothing. Only–' She's crouching over it wiping it with the palm of her hand. Then she dabs it with a corner of her shirt.

As she does so Kelly squeals with delight.

'Ooh! Lucy Bresslaw! You little slag! You *showed* him. You're a sly one.' Kelly turns to me.

'So what do you think about *that*, Frankie? Eh?'

'What *are* you on about?' I feel guilty about the book even if it is old. I don't want it, do I, but I'm sorry it got dropped. But it's not the end of the world. I just wish Lucy would leave me alone. These little kids are so annoying. They get in the way when all I want to do is watch Emilia. And it's not just me. Everybody is fascinated by her. Nobody can leave her alone. It's like flies on . . . jam, someone said yesterday. Well, they didn't say 'jam' actually, but something else, but I know what they meant.

'See?' Kelly lunges at Lucy and pulls up the corner of her school skirt. And there it is on her skinny white stomach and it's really horrid. She's had her belly button pierced. It is just gross and I'm relieved when she grabs back the edge of her shirt and jams it into her trousers again, so that the beastly thing is covered up.

'What do you think then?' teases Kelly. 'She did it for *you*, lover boy.'

'I didn't!' screams Lucy. 'You're a liar, Kelly. I did it . . . for *me*. *I* like it. So there!'

'OK, OK,' Kelly mocks. 'I'll believe you, though thousands wouldn't.'

'It's true,' shrieks Lucy again.

'About that book,' I begin. Lucy's face is red with held-in tears.

Out of the corner of my eye I've noticed Ian walking towards us.

'Here. Have it.' Lucy slips the book back into my hands. She smiles. Somehow all that anger has slid from her face like butter across a hot plate. There's no mistake this time. She doesn't want her father to know.

'Everything all right here?' Ian asks pleasantly. We all nod. I'm working the book deep into my pocket.

'You coming home, Dad? Lucy asks brightly.

'Not yet, love. But you carry on.'

'OK. See you.' She jumps up and dusts herself down. She's humming loudly as she skips out of the school gate. She's humming as if she hasn't a care in the world. Kelly sniffs back scorn.

Luckily I'm going in the opposite direction. Halfway to Mrs Seagrove's I remember Lucy's words: 'she said you could have this'. She must have spoken to her mother recently, visited, actually, to have got this book from her. So when did she go and why had they talked about me? This is peculiar. Why should this artist, this Alicia, who's stayed in the country miles from anywhere, why should she want to send a book for *me*? You'd think I'd be the last person she'd help. After all, my mum is 'the other woman', isn't she? I'm the son of the woman who's seeing her husband. Doesn't she care?

Outside Mrs Seagrove's I take another look. It's *Lamb's Tales from Shakespeare*, whatever that is. And it's old. Her name is inside the front cover in round blue ink: 'Alicia Fontwell, Lower 5th'. It's her old school book. She's kept it all this time, only to give it to me. Or has she? What if Lucy nicked it to impress me? She might have, mightn't she, if that stuff about the piercing was true? She might have pinched this book. It's pathetic. And if she's done it for me it's really disgusting. It's like she's trying to *buy* my affection. Next time I see her I'll tell her what her tummy button really looks like: some nasty, fat maggot coiled up in there and going off. That should shut her up and put an end to her stupid ideas, if she has them. I doubt it, actually, because Kelly Jackson is a drama queen. She'll say anything to get attention. Everybody knows that.

Mrs Seagrove is taking ages to answer my knock. I know she's home because the curtain twitches.

'Oh!' she says, opening the door, 'it's you again.'

'Yes. If that's all right . . . '

'If you must,' she mutters grudgingly. But she's been expecting me because things have been tidied up. There are six fancy biscuits arranged on a crumpled doily on a plate.

'Well,' she says, 'do you want your tea before or after, because I don't want you spilling things.'

'After?' I guess. Somehow it seems safest because I *am* clumsy sometimes. She takes the biscuits away and puts them up high and I'm just wondering what on earth she expects me to do, when Snowy flounces in and scowls at me. She must have just had her tea because there's a bit of something meaty still stuck on her moustache. It reminds me that I wouldn't have minded a biscuit after all.

'Of course,' Mrs Seagrove says unexpectedly, stroking Snowy's head, 'they don't like cats. Horses, yes, but not cats. Oh no. They won't even touch a cat: because they're dirty and lick. That's why they don't like 'em.'

'Who don't?' I'm confused.

'Gypsies of course! 'Ere, I thought that was why you come? For the gypsies. If it isn't, you'd better go, because I've got things to be getting on with.'

Then I notice the box of old photos on the straightened sofa.

'That's him,' she nods. 'That's my Ernie.' She picks one out.

The edges of this old black-and-white photo are scalloped and the paper is stiff and yellowed. I take it from her very carefully. It's a portrait of a young man. He's looking back at us seriously, but not directly, somehow. He's staring over my shoulder at something too far away, and his eyes are narrowed. One hand rests on the smooth head of the skinny mongrel beside him. He's wearing a hat, tipped at an angle.

'Mr Jones took that,' she says, in a quieter voice. 'For me. He sent it specially, in the post.'

'Mr Jones?'

'That's right. Mr Jones the tallyman, what was in the hop fields with all of us. He took that snap. People like us didn't have nothing like cameras did we, in those days? But that Mr Jones did photography like. He took hundreds of photos, for the record, he said. He was that keen and he sent that one to me. Afterwards like, as a keepsake. When he heard about my Ernie and what happened.'

It's very quiet in the room and too warm. She must have had the little bar fire on for ages. I almost ask what *did* happen, but I don't, even though I've barely understood anything she's said.

'There,' she says, putting another photo into my hand. 'That's what it was like in the old days. Before the war.' She turns it over. We peer at the faint date pencilled on the back: 1938. It's a photo of a crowd of people working in a hop field.

'1938,' she murmurs. We're sitting either side of the box. 'I was sixteen that year. Sixteen in the April. There! See? That's me. At the back there. That's me.' And it is too. She was a plumpish girl, quite big, really, in a dress or a skirt with a belt and a sort of jacket. Her hair was dark then.

In the photo I can see that the vines have been cut down from the overhead wires. Now this group of people are stripping the hops into one of the bins. I understand it because we did a project about the Kentish hopfields in school. Nowadays the work is all mechanized but before the Second World War it was done by hand. Pickers used to come down from London. Each September they'd travel out of the East End of London to the farms in Kent for the harvest. Whole families came and everybody worked. It was the nearest thing to a holiday that most of them ever got. When we did the project a couple of old ladies came into school and told us all about it. They brought stuff too, like the tally sticks, for counting up how many bins you'd filled. One of them showed us the letters with the bin tickets which the hop farmers sent to the pickers each year, inviting them back, if they'd been good workers.

I look at the photo more closely. Yes. It really is her. She's just a girl with her head on one side and her hair all straggly. Now she's leaning over to point out her mum and dad, her aunts and uncles, her best friend Peg, who's got great sticking-out teeth. Those, she says, were next-door neighbours and they used to come down all together on special trains from London.

I want to ask loads of questions but I'm afraid it'll distract her. Old people are like that. They suddenly start talking about something else all together and it's usually as boring as anything.

'About the gypsies,' I begin. 'You said–'

'I didn't say nothing against no gypsies,' she looks up sharply. Fiercely, almost. I see the girl she was: a strong girl, standing her ground, working from morning till evening in the hop fields, her hands and arms scratched and stained by the torn-away stems. That's what the other old ladies complained of: the smell of the hops. It stayed with them for weeks, they said, and turned their hands brown.

'I didn't mean that,' I mutter.

'It's your mother, her and that Liz Quiggley what you should be talking to. Not me,' she snaps tartly.

I don't know what to say. I finger through more photos. Here she is again, but different. Now she's in a sort of uniform, standing beside another girl, and her straggly hair is cut and smoothed and waved. I don't like to look too closely: she's almost beautiful.

'That's me,' she relaxes, 'and that's my friend Peg again. She joined up with me. Afterwards. Didn't tell our mothers, either of us. We just joined up, lied about everything we did then, only it wasn't real lies, was it? Not in those days. You do it for your country, don't you, when there's a war on? Everybody joined up. Like he did. Or wanted to.'

Snowy jumps up. You wouldn't think such a fat cat could jump, but she does and settles into Mrs Seagrove's lap. And licks. She sticks out one bedraggled white leg and licks happily.

'That's why, you see,' says Mrs Seagrove.

I nod, but I don't see at all.

'And you can see how there's sense in it, can't you? Not entirely, but a bit of sense, because it's not so nice is it, to be licking away and swallowing your own dirt, like that! But that's cats for you.'

We're both watching the animal, listening to the sound of its rough tongue teasing apart the soiled white fluff.

'People think,' she begins, 'ignorant people that is, think

92

that gypsies themselves is dirty, but it's not true. It's not like that at all. It's just that . . . they think different from us, and very particular: gypsies can't have what's clean mixed with what's unclean, like cats do. Cats lick their dirty outside and it goes into them and . . . and dirties them . . . pollutes them, that's what they say nowadays, don't they, on the telly. It's all about this pollution and spoiling things. Well, that was what my Ernie believed all that time ago. He didn't think things should be spoiled by all the modern ways.

'That's why the gypsies had different bowls for washing clothes and dishes. If you muddled them up, let them touch even, you had to throw them away. Even if they were brand new. Of course, I'd have learnt all that: he'd have taught me. Only there wasn't time, was there, with the war coming so sudden that summer, and my Ernie going away like that. And not coming back. That's why, afterwards, Mr Jones sent me the photo. He said I needed something, apart from my memories. He was a proper gent: an educated man, with books what he lent to folk, despite being tallyman for the hoppers.'

Snowy stretches out her claws and darts her pink tongue between the pads.

'They was such lovely people, the gypsies. Not all of them, mind you, and some wouldn't even talk to you, thought you was rubbish or worse, but my Ernie wasn't like that. Nor his dad. They was *so* good to me. Better than my folks ever was.' She shakes her head slowly, as though it's a puzzle even now. 'My dad . . . ' She shakes her head again. 'It wasn't all toffee with my dad.'

Snowy begins to purr and I think I can hear water boiling.

'Shall I make the tea?'

'Yes dear. That'd be nice.' She's stroking the cat rhythmically. 'If you can manage, that is.'

I do and I carry in the tray that she's left ready. I pour out so she doesn't have to disturb the cat. She blows across the top of her cup, sips noisily and smiles over the edge.

'Now tuck in. A growing lad like you needs to keep your strength up.' I take a tiny, bright pink wafer – and choke. I can't stop coughing or get my breath. I'm spraying out bits of wafer. Snowy leaps up, knocks the cup from Mrs Seagrove's hand and there's scalding tea and bits of broken china everywhere.

'Oh dear, she says, grimly, 'can't your family do anything right?'

11

Evening

Nobody's home when I get in. I put the telly on for a bit of noise, settle into the armchair and take the book out of my pocket. Luckily the tea missed it. It smells of old, undusted shelves and some of the pages are marked with little brown spots like freckles.

She's like that. I noticed it a couple of days ago when she smiled at me during lunch. Her freckles are scattered over the bridge of her nose like a faint dusting of pollen. Emilia often smiles now. In fact, she smiles a lot, though she never did at first. In school people smile back at her because they can't talk about anything. So they grin. It's crazy really and anyway people are crazy about her. It's as if she's a princess or a super model or someone important. They can't leave her alone.

When she said 'hello' to me and smiled, that's when I noticed her freckles. She says 'hello' to everyone but I think it was a bit different when she said it to me. Her voice was special, though nobody else noticed. She has a low voice, not exactly gruff, because girls' voices aren't, but hers is scratchy, or hoarse, like after a cough. When she said 'hello' to me in that voice I felt as though something had crawled under my collar and down the back of my neck. I could feel it fluttering about on my spine. I loosened my tie and had to scratch. She tossed her plaits over her shoulder and shrugged as she poked her fork into the school meal on her tray. Sam was sitting with us but he didn't notice a thing.

I turn over some pages: *Lamb's Tales from Shakespeare*. But this is a children's book. It isn't the real thing at all. Trust Lucy to get it wrong. This book explains the complicated plots of Shakespeare's plays to children. It even says as much in the introduction. And there are illustrations, so it must be for pretty dumb kids too! *Othello* is on page 57. It's not a very good picture, and it isn't even of Desdemona. If I'd been illustrating the play I'd have done the scene where Othello strangles Desdemona, or smothers her, I can't remember which it is, but I'd have made it pretty exciting with her squirming on the bed and her legs kicking about. That's how they do strangling on films. This book only has a picture of Iago holding that stupid handkerchief. Behind him a distant ship sails on a blue sea, well, it's a galley more than a ship, isn't it, with rows of golden oars. In the foreground old Iago is clutching this frilly handkerchief. He's looking at it like he's picked up a bit of dog poo, to be honest. I've seen people in the park with that fixed grin, holding their pooper-scoopers out in front of them, though most of them don't bother and you step right in it. Anyway, here Iago's got this glazed grin and his eyes are staring. It's a really nasty expression, as if he's had a sniff, and liked it, in a sick sort of way.

I read on a bit. I suppose it's not bad. I don't need plots explained for me, but someone like Sam might. I can see that it could help him. He'd be able to understand the

storyline and enjoy the illustrations too. He's into pictures –
and graffiti: I've seen him from the balcony. In school he's
always doodling. Mum says he ought to do something like
that for a living: be a painter and decorator maybe, because
you don't need exams to make a living at that. Mum wants
me to go to university. Everybody goes now, she says. Last
year somebody from our school went to Oxford or Cam-
bridge or somewhere extra good, the first one ever, and it
was in the local paper and announced in Assembly. I might
do that, if I feel like it. Nobody in my family has ever been
to university. I don't think anybody's ever done A Levels
even, though Ian says there's no reason why not. He seems
to think Lucy will go, but I don't. Lucy hasn't got what it
takes. Imagine digging a hole in your own belly button! I
don't think that's at all intelligent.

I read *Romeo and Juliet* after *Othello*. The illustration for this
is of 'the ball in Verona' – at least that's what the caption
says. I haven't read the play but I saw the film last year. Mum
took me and cried buckets. I thought it was a bit wet but she
said I didn't understand because I wasn't 'mature enough'.
She's mistaken, because I understood perfectly. I just didn't
think it was that good, but I wouldn't mind seeing it again. I
bet Mrs Morris has the video in the library. I'll borrow it
tomorrow and then I could ask a few people round to watch
it, couldn't I? Not Lucy, obviously, because she *is* too young
and immature, but sensible people like Yasmina and Arshad.
Maybe Katy Morris would come, even though she's not in
my class, and Sam, I suppose, because he's near. I don't
think he ever does stuff like that. And I could ask Emilia,
couldn't I? I could get Yasmina to bring her because
apparently they live near each other on the High Street. I'd

walk them both home afterwards. It would be really special for Emilia. I could even make a cake or do pizza.

Only I can't, can I? Not with Mum. I can hear her now: 'It's not that I've anything against her *personally*, I'm sure she's a really nice girl, but it's the principle of the thing, isn't it, Frankie? If we let one family in then all the others will follow won't they? We'll be swamped. We won't be able to cope. Everybody wants to come here, don't they. And you can't blame them.' Sometimes she looks upset when she talks about these immigrants, as if it hurts her to say these things. She says *she* has to do it, because nobody else will. Somebody has to speak out.

But sometimes I just wish she'd bloody well shut up. I'm sick of it, even though it isn't anything to do with me. It's not that I think Mum's wrong exactly. It's just that I wish she'd keep quiet. I mean there are councils and laws for this sort of thing, as well as MPs. It should be *their* job. What's more, I never get any peace: our phone never stops ringing. Mum bought an answering machine last week, but the phone still rings, doesn't it?

Mum's even doing an interview with the local rag. Her and Liz Quiggley, which is *such* a laugh. Mum says Liz Quiggley is 'making a real effort' and that I should be more understanding. It must be a good thing, mustn't it, if Liz makes an effort? It's just a shame she doesn't make her effort with Sam. He hasn't improved at all. That boy smells awful when he's been by the radiator a bit. I've mentioned it, sort of, but he doesn't take the hint. He still pongs. I use deodorant and breath freshener. I keep them in my school bag, just in case. Lots of guys do. Except Sam. I'm sure Emilia minds when she sits beside him, but *she* can't say anything, can she? Actually she still doesn't say much at all, just 'hello' and 'yes' and 'Emilia'. She does that a lot, she points at herself, laying her hand on her neck and sort of asking. 'Emilia?' she says, in that scratching voice, meaning 'shall I come too?' or 'do I do that as well?' and when we nod, she does it. But I'm sure she'll learn English really quickly, even though somebody said she's never even been to school before. Not in Romania. It wasn't allowed, apparently, for gypsies. No wonder she doesn't understand about the uniform.

There's a bit in *Othello* where Iago speaks about how an ideal woman should be. He says:

She that could think and ne'er disclose her mind,
See suitors following and not look behind.

That could describe our Emilia: I'm sure she knows things, but doesn't need to say them. And she must understand that all these people are crazy about her, but she never 'looks behind'. They say that about gypsies, don't they, that they *know* things . . . secrets and stuff, but that they never let on. They even have their own secret language.

A key turns in our lock. It's only Ian. I'm put out. I thought he was going home to Lucy. Recently he's started ringing the bell again or knocking first, though he's had a key for months. I didn't want him to have one but Mum said that he was almost family and couldn't be hanging around outside, not in Poet's Rise. I don't see it myself. It might do him good to hang around a bit.

'Hard at it!' he quips, dropping his jacket on the floor. I wish he'd hang it up. He's such a slob.

'No!' I read on.

'Do you mind?' He turns the TV off.

'I do actually. I was *watching* that,' I snarl.

'You weren't. You were reading.'

'I was doing *both*.'

'Fine.' But he doesn't turn it back on. So I do. And *I've* got the remote. I push past and press the button. The set fizzes and leaps back. I zap the sound up from the safety of the armchair. He goes into the kitchen. Now I can't concentrate at all. He's getting things out, saucepans and stuff, and that's rice tipped into a sieve and washed. He doesn't half clatter.

'There's no need,' I yell. '*I'm* doing tea tonight.'

He's carrying on. He's such a know-all, such a poser.

'I said *I'd* do it, Ian! Mum asked *me*!'

'What? Put that thing *off*, for Christ's sake, Frankie. I can't hear myself think–'

'Big loss.'

He looks at me.

'I couldn't hear you either,' he says.

'You don't have to.'

He's still looking at me. I know what he'll say next. It'll be 'what's up?' or something and in a really calm sympathetic voice. I hate that. And I hate him being here. I just wish he'd bugger off, go, vanish, be knocked down by a bus if necessary. I know Mum would be upset, but it would be for the best, in the end. And it would be such a relief. I wouldn't mind cooking tea for her every evening. Then perhaps she'd give up on the gypsies – because I did wonder if she was doing it partly to impress him, to show him that *she* has intelligent ideas too.

'How's Alicia then?' I ask.

He's gobsmacked, winded as if I've punched him in the stomach. I'm gutted too. It just sprang out of my mouth. As soon as it's said I'm excited because I know I'm on to something. He still can't manage a reply. But I'll wait.

I hold the book out. He looks more puzzled. I've got him on the run. He blinks as he reads the name. His wife's name.

'Does Mum know?' I ask.

'Yes – no. Not about our last visit – but it wasn't like that. It *isn't* like that, Frankie. Lucy has to see her mother. *Wants* to see her mother, obviously. And I take her. Godmersham's right in the country. She can't get there on her own!' He's getting worked up, defending himself. 'But there's nothing between us – Alicia and me. There's nothing going on, I promise you, Frankie. I wouldn't mess your mother around. Or you. Believe me.'

But I don't. And I don't answer either. I lower the sound and turn a page and pretend to be engrossed. He hovers. But he doesn't know that I can't concentrate on anything, does he? He fiddles with his watch. Maybe he's beginning to wise up; maybe he realizes that I'm on his case.

It's the best meal he's ever cooked: sushi, followed by fresh mangoes caramelized under the grill. Mum is delighted. Overwhelmed, really, and her eyes keep meeting his over the bunch of carnations which he hastily puts on the table. We're quiet though. All of us. Mum mentions it but Lucy, who's come round too and brought those flowers, explains straightaway:

'I think it's Dad's cooking, isn't it? It's so stunning. Much better than he ever does for me at home! I just want to eat and eat.' She smiles at Mum and Mum smiles back, then

101

spikes the last prawn, dips it in sauce and offers it to Ian. Lucy looks away, but I don't. I watch them, because I know what this meal is really about. It's a bribe, isn't it? He's been seeing his wife again and he wants me to shut up. He doesn't want me to tell Mum. Well I won't. Not yet, anyway. I watch him open his thin lips and take the prawn off the fork, and chew.

'June?' He asks.

'Mmm?' Her voice is softer than usual, warmer too, after the wine.

'Will you do something for me?'

She blinks, her huge eyes suddenly alert.

'I've already talked to Lucy about it and she knows what I'm going to say–' Lucy's nodding proudly. Nobody looks at me.

'I want to take you away, June, for Christmas and New Year. I want us to have a week's holiday together. The four of us.' Now he glances at me. 'I've made a booking, provisionally mind, for a week in Paris. A friend has opened a small hotel–' he jumps up and gets the brochure from the kitchen. Lucy's eyes are glowing. Mum is biting her lip. She turns the pages. He leans over her shoulder and kisses her neck.

'Say yes, June.'

Mum takes another sip of wine.

'Yes.'

Lucy jumps up and kisses Ian and looks as if she's going to kiss Mum too.

'But Mum,' I yell. 'You *can't* go. What about the campaign? You can't just walk out on it like that. What'll people think?'

12

....

Monday morning

'Well,' Sam mutters, 'I think you're mad. Barking, I'd say.
Absolutely bloody barking.'

'I agree.' Arshad nods vigorously. I frown at him: he's
always sticking his nose in where it isn't wanted.

'A free week in France,' he puffs out his cheeks, 'and in a
hotel, for Chrissake, and you turn it down! You need your
head looking at.' He glances round the changing room and
sniffs at the old, cold steam from the showers. 'So what's so
great about this dump that you don't want to go to Paris,
man? I mean . . . Paris!'

We're getting dressed after the Monday morning run. I'm
dragging damp socks over damp feet and it's not what I
want to hear. I wish I hadn't told them now. Actually I
never did tell Arshad. He just tagged along when Sam and I
nipped through the short cut behind Woolworth's. Then he
earwigged.

'I mean,' Arshad groans, 'what's with Christmas anyway?
There's nothing decent on telly and all my relatives come
and it's not even our thing is it? I'm supposed to be a
Muslim, aren't I!' He snorts. 'The whole house is full of

103

toddlers and their mothers. It smells of them and their nappies. It's not like when we were young.'

We all nod wisely like very old men. Then the other two turn on me again.

'He's right,' mumbles Sam, 'you don't know what a good thing is. You never have.'

'What do you mean?'

'I mean about Bresslaw. He's all right, he is. You should be glad your mum's got a bloke like him, Frankie. You think he's a pain, but I can tell you, you don't know what real pain is! You've got it made, you have, but you don't even know it!'

I stare. Sam's never said so much in one go. And I can't think why he's bothered now because all I did was tell him that Ian wanted to take Mum and me to France with him but that I wasn't keen.

'And I'll tell you something else,' adds Arshad: 'your mum might just up and go without you.'

'She wouldn't!' I scoff because he doesn't know June. 'No way!' Though to be honest, I suddenly wish she would. I'd like a week on my own. Then I'd get a bit of peace.

I can picture it: the door shutting behind Mum and the sound of her car driving off on Christmas Eve. She would have shed a tear, begged me to change my mind. But I wouldn't. And I wouldn't be lonely either. Nor sulk. No way. I'd run a huge, hot bath and just lie in it for a bit, letting the water get deeper and deeper. Then I'd put on clean things and go out into the bright night looking really smart because I'd lost weight after running. Everything would be open and lit up because of Christmas shopping. The Salvation Army would be playing hymns, but this year

104

it would be jolly with folk smiling and joining in. I'd take my savings out of the cash machine. Not all of it, but enough, say, and I'd fold this crisp wad of new notes into my wallet.

Then I'd meet her of course, casually, like by accident. Her face would glow when she saw me. We'd look around a bit, our shoulders touching. There'd be one Christmas tree left on its own and I'd buy it and some Christmas food and I'd carry it all in my arms, even the holly and the mistletoe. She'd want to help, but I wouldn't let her, so she'd just smile at me with her eyes sparkling like stars. I'd give her one of her presents early because she'd be cold. I'd drape this beautiful soft scarf around her head and neck. It'd be red of course, a dark, pinky red and she would stop shivering, wouldn't she, with my scarf around her. Then she'd walk home at my side and people would see us and smile mistily. Mrs Seagrove would call 'Happy Christmas' from her window. We'd go over and she'd wipe a tear from her cheek. 'Why,' she'd say, 'don't you two make a picture', because I'd have the tree under my arm and Emilia would be looking beautiful and excited because this was her first proper Christmas ever. It might even snow. Big white flakes would drift down and . . . and . . . on to the red scarf . . .

'It's no fun,' says Sam doggedly. He's wiped a mirror clean and is staring at himself. 'No fun at all.'

'What isn't?'

'Being on your own at Christmas.'

'Oh.' Now Arshad and I stare but we don't know what to say to him.

Sam's smoothing down his hair: not combing it, just flattening it with his hands.

'Anyway,' chirps up Arshad, 'Frankie's not planning on being on his own.'

'What do you mean?' I ask. He winks. I grin.

'Our Frankie's got other plans if you ask me. Once Mum's off the scene, he's planning a party! Eh Frankie? A little *Christmas* party? For . . . two?'

'No!' But I want to say yes. I can't help grinning more.

'And do you know which party games they're going to play?' Arshad asks, choking with laughter. Sam shakes his head. 'One's called "padding palms"!'

'Eh?' Sam looks up.

'It's Shakespeare,' I explain. *'Othello.'*

'I *know* it's Shakespeare!' Sam scowls. He's even paler than usual. He's white with anger and I don't know why.

Sam swings round from the mirror. 'You bastard,' he yells and comes for us. I duck. His arm misses and he runs off. Then I understand what it's about: he's sticking up for *me*, for me and Emilia. He's a real mate. He doesn't want Arshad to repeat all that stuff about couples that the lads say. He wanted to shut Arshad up. And that's brilliant. It means that people *know* about me and her – that people recognize that me and her are . . . well . . . are going to be . . . an item. Sort of a couple.

I know I'm grinning terrifically now but I don't care because I'm just so happy. Suddenly everything is all right again or better than all right. And I'm wondering if there's still time to dash up to the library. I'll get the *Romeo and Juliet* video out. If everyone knows how I feel about Emilia, Mum will just have to shut up, won't she? She can't stop me doing what I want. Not now. Not when it's official. So she'd better get used to it. I'm not a kid any longer. She owes me that. After all, I've put up with blokes she's fancied. I even put up with Brian. So she really owes me.

'Francis!' It's Barry and he's yelling. 'Are you *deaf* as well as lazy?'

'No, sir.'

'Then *move* it! Now!'

I'm alone. Arshad's gone too. It's just Barry and me and a litter of dropped gear and splashes of mud. The swing door has slapped shut and I can hear the squeaking tread of wet shoes hurrying along the corridor. I suppose the bell must have rung, but I never noticed. I feel a bit put out. Sam and Arshad might have warned me instead of disappearing like that.

'Well?' he storms as I put my deodorant back in my bag.

'I'm going. I'm on my way.'

He looks at me then.

'Good,' he says, but quietly now. He's watching me but his mood has changed. It's as cold and quiet as sudden winter fog. 'Good. Because I'm telling you, Francis: just between you and me, the day I thought that people like you were finally going on their way out of Poet's Rise, that's the day when decent folk could sleep soundly in their beds. If you get my point.'

I don't. But he's gone anyway: he's stomped off as if I'm, well, nothing. Nothing at all. The bloody drunken fool. Because that's what's caused this outburst, obviously. It's like Mum says: he's just a drunk and he's forgotten who my mother is. He's as drunk as Cassio and as stupid.

I'm late for English. Quite late, it seems because they're all bent over their tables, writing. It looks like a test. Mrs Rushmoor is pacing up and down the rows, checking.

Nobody has seen me looking in, which is lucky, because I've noticed that Emilia isn't in class either. She's probably got lost again. She does, often. People are always finding her in the wrong room. She's usually sitting patiently, drawing stuff on scraps of paper.

I step back from the door. No. No one has seen me. So I know what I'll do. I'll find her and bring her back safely. It'll also cover up why I'm late. I'll go via the library. Then I can ask about *Romeo and Juliet*. Actually I wouldn't have minded doing the test. I usually do well. I've got into *Othello* now. I'd know all the answers.

And then I hear her laugh. She's not in the corridor but I know it's her. I'd know her voice, her laugh anywhere: it's like . . . like something touched inside me. Like nothing else in the world. It makes me gasp for breath. And want to feel where she is.

The corridor is empty. Far away there's the thud and jump of people in the gym. Here it's quiet. I can hear the drone from the language lab, like bees or interference on the phone. And then her laugh again.

'Now I?' she cries, and laughs once more.

'Emilia?' I call.

Silence, but somewhere, something moves.

'Emilia?' Slowly I open the door to the Art Room. I don't want to startle her. She's by the board.

'Emilia, it's English. *Eng–glish*. In Room 4. Now.' I point to my watch and repeat it all slowly and clearly.

She has her back to the board which is half covered in drawings.

'Come on.' I hold the door open for her.

She snatches up the duster and begins to rub off the work.

'Don't!' I cry. 'Don't, Emilia. No!'

She's probably wiping off a lesson but in her panic she drops the duster. It clatters down in clouds of dust. I don't want her to destroy any more; I don't want her to get into trouble.

'You shouldn't, Emilia, honestly.' Maybe she thinks she had to clean things up. I think that's what they made people like her do where she's come from. Somebody told me that last week: that in Romania they made gypsies do the cleaning and collect rubbish and stuff.

'Emilia–' I catch hold of her wrist as she grabs the duster.

Then she hits me. She slaps me across my face. I let go instantly. I wasn't trying to hold on to her anyway. I only wanted to stop her doing more damage. I'm only trying to help her, but I can't now because my eyes are watering too much. I think my nose is bleeding.

'Don't, Emilia!' I protest. 'Don't rub them off.'

'Why not?' It's Sam. 'Why not, you prat!' He gives me a shove. I fall against the side of a table. He runs at me. I try to get out of the way and the table goes over. All the tins of paint and trays and jars of brushes clatter down and smash over us both. I sneeze. Powder paints have gone up my nose.

'Don't!' Sam's white with fury and his face is touching mine. I can see flecks of bright green spittle on his lips. The stumps of his teeth are decayed and black. 'Don't,' he spits into my mouth, 'don't *ever* touch her again. You or your mother. Or I'll . . . I'll–' He's choking. I'm trying to push him off but can't even though he's so skinny, because he's mad, absolutely mad.

Barry pulls us apart. There's a crowd at the door. There

always is for a fight. Mrs Morris appears, clapping her hands, shooing people back into their classrooms.

'Show's over kids,' says Barry. His T-shirt is blotched with paint, and one eyebrow is orange. But nobody's laughing. Sam shakes himself free. His shirt is ripped. I need to get up too but can't.

Mrs Morris comes over to help me. She glances down at me, but steps straight over my legs. I can smell her perfume amongst the blood and paint. But she isn't putting her arms round me. She's putting them right around Emilia. She's hugging her tight. I can see her hand, with the beautiful ring, smoothe down the fair hair. She's stroking Emilia's forehead, laying the plaits straight across her back. Somewhere there's broken glass. I can hear it crunch. A tin is kicked and rolls across the floor.

I feel a bit odd actually. I begin to get up, then sway a bit. For one very hot moment the edges of the room darken as though the spilt paint is floating around in the air and blinding me.

'Steady on old man.' It's Ian Bresslaw, but not his usual voice. 'Up you get. That's it. Slowly now. You've just banged your head. That's all.' He pushes me down into a chair. He might have been talking to a little kid but he isn't. He's talking to me. I put my hand to my forehead. There's a huge lump there. It's beginning to hurt. It's so enormous: egg-sized at least. Mum'll go spare. I look around for Sam and Emilia, but they've gone now. There's no one here at all. Just me and Ian and on the board the remains of the picture that she was trying to rub out.

13

....

Midday

'Take your time,' says Ian. 'Then for heaven's sake, Frankie,
tell me what this is all about.'

'Nothing. It's not about anything. It's a stupid mistake.'

'Don't give me that!' He sounds tired, bored almost.

'It's true. Sam made a mistake. He didn't mean to hit me.
He got confused. He does. You don't know him like I do. It's
because he's a Quiggley. He's–'

'This isn't about Sam Quiggley. It's about you, Francis.
You. And I'm trying to give you a chance to explain. So talk
to me. Please. I'm trying to help!'

'Then don't.'

'Francis,' he sighs, 'you're in big trouble here.'

'Me?'

I've never been in trouble in my life. No way. Ian's got it
all wrong.

'Yes. *You*. For crying out loud Frankie, you hit that girl–'

'I didn't! I was trying to stop her. Who says I hit her?
They're lying. I was *helping*. Anyway she hit *me* – only it
wasn't like that. She didn't mean it either. She–'

The art room slides slowly to one side. I blink. It steadies

111

itself. My head really does hurt. I try to focus on the board, on the pictures. I need to see them clearly.

'Francis? Are you OK?'

The stupid git. Of course I'm not OK.

She's rubbed out most of Poet's Rise but one block remains. Or part of it. There's a figure beside it. A little person, chalk white, with shaky stick-thin legs and arms held up. And hair . . . trailing down . . . almost to the ground.

I blink again and finger the lump. It's even bigger now, and hot. There's blood on my hand, dried blood around my nails, but I'm concentrating on the picture. One of the art teachers must have drawn it. Then I notice the flames. Red flames are bursting from the gashed block: red as red with sharp, jealous lines of yellow here and there. The chalk figure stands below, looking up, reaching up.

Ian walks me to the cloakroom to clean up before taking me in to the Deputy Head. People go quiet when they see me. Their jaws drop. One or two crack up. When I come face to face with myself in the mirror I understand why: I'm splattered all over. I could have been an advert for a paint-ball game. I try a joke about that with Ian but he doesn't lighten up. He finds some spare games kit, chucks it over and tells me to get on with it. I can't think why he's taking such an interest. I'm not in his tutor group or his history set. I'm nothing to do with him. I expect it's to suck up to Mum. I wish he'd just back off.

'Ah. Francis. Francis Johnson?'

The Axe had read my name from the pad on her desk. I'm a bit surprised. I thought she knew me. She takes off her glasses and looks across at me. She must be able to see the lump but she doesn't mention it; doesn't even ask me how I am. She's tough. Seriously tough. Everybody knows that.

'We've contacted your mother, Francis, and asked her to come in, but she says she can't. Not right away. She said she's in the middle of a perm–'

I don't like her tone. She shouldn't speak about Mum in that dismissive way.

'My mother's a hairdresser, Miss. She can't just walk out and leave them. She's the manager.'

'I see.'

'And anyway, I'm fine. I don't need my mother here. It'll upset her. She doesn't like upsets. She doesn't need to come.'

'Oh but she does, Francis. She needs to know what's been happening.'

'Nothing's been happening. Honestly, Miss Chester. It's all a mistake. It's . . . it's . . . I can explain.'

'Can you?' At least she lets me try. She takes me through it step by step and writes it down. In the end I think she's beginning to understand. Apparently she's already spoken to Sam. And to Ian. I can't believe that. It's such a cheek. Ian's got no right to talk about me behind my back. Who's he to play the good parent when all the time he's cheating on my mum! And he leaves his daughter all alone at night. I bet old Axe-face doesn't know about that. I don't tell her of course. You never can, and even when you do, no one listens.

Mum steps into the office. She sees me, and gasps. Her face crumples. She looks tired and small and shabby. There are snippets of hair on her tights and skirt. She must have finished that perm and driven straight round. I feel upset seeing her here. I'm touched, sort of, but I still wish she hadn't come.

She lays two fingers lightly on the lump.

'Has he seen the doctor yet?' she demands.

'I don't need a doctor.'

'Not need a doctor! With something like that on your head? Who did it, Miss Chester? Who did that to Francis, because it wasn't there this morning. I don't send my son to school to be beaten up, you know!'

I knew she shouldn't have come. They sit her down and bring in a cup of tea. The school nurse takes me away to lie down with a jumbo packet of frozen peas on my head. I feel a bit of a prat: the sick bay is always full of girls clutching hot-water bottles and complaining of period pains. Today, however, only one other patient comes in. It's Katy, Mrs Morris's granddaughter. Just my luck.

'What's up?' I croak from under the peas. I think they're freezing my tongue as well as my face. She doesn't reply for a moment. She looks embarrassed. Maybe it is her period. Then she holds out a finger.

'Splinter. Present from the gym.' She laughs in an awkward way and doesn't ask about me. So does *she* know? Or is she just being . . . tactful? I can imagine that she would be. People like her are diplomatic: they don't blurt out everything, do they? Not like Mum. June usually says the first thing that comes into her head. Unfortunately. But maybe it's more honest that way. And dangerous.

I'm pretty uncomfortable thinking about her upstairs with the Axe. It's taking ages. Maybe they're discussing school business. After all Mum is a parent governor.

'Katy?' I remember the video. Maybe she could borrow it

for me. I don't think I'll have time now. I'd like to watch it even if Mum doesn't go off to Paris. I'll still invite Sam. I want to show him I don't hold a grudge, because it *really* wasn't anything. He got the wrong end of the stick. It's because of his family whatever Ian thinks. It's the Quiggley way: they lose their tempers and explode. The only thing is I've never known Sam do that. Until now, Sam has always been the quiet one.

Mum puts her head round the san door.

'Come on you!' Her face is . . . old. Lined like paper scrunched up. Katy stares at us, then blushes. She's remembering what she said in the hall. And I know what else. I know exactly what she's thinking: 'Is that pathetic woman really your *mother*?' She bends her thin, white neck over and inspects the splinter. She'd rather look at that than at us and it makes me cringe. I hand the peas back to the nurse and we leave, Mum and I, in total silence. Nobody says anything at all.

Mum doesn't speak until we are home.

'How *could* you, Francis!' she wails, as soon as we're inside. 'How could you do this to me?'

'Do *what*?' I'm getting worked up too. This isn't fair. I'm the one who got hurt.

'How could you get in a fight over . . . a girl like that . . . over a *gypsy*, a . . . a . . . ' She's so angry she can't speak. I can't either.

We're standing close, almost touching in the narrow hall. Her froggy face is turned up to mine. Her pop eyes bulge with fury. I try to push past. I want to get to my room. I want to shut the door but she won't let me.

'I'm telling you, Francis. I've *never* been so ashamed in all

115

my life. Never! Nobody's ever spoken to me like that woman did. Not even when I was a cleaner. People have always shown me respect. But that Miss Chester! She's a dried-up old bitch, that's what she is. I could see it at once. And twisted too. Asking *me* about *my* life as though it's got anything to do with it. Looking for motives in people. It's unhealthy, that's what it is. Fancy saying that it was *my* responsibility: as though *I* brought these people here. And for you to get mixed up with that girl!'

'I'm–'

'Don't you lie to me. I knew it all along! I *knew* something was up, the way you never stop talking about her. "Emilia this" and "Emilia that" – she must be a right little madam to get you hooked the way she has! What's she done, eh? Shown you a good time? The little slut. That's what I told your Miss Chester. These girls are brought up different: they don't have our morals. They can't. Girls like her are married at twelve, thirteen, they don't know any better. Then they flood in over here and the government gives them every-thing *free*: houses, and social security, and they think they can run rings round the rest of us. I told her, but she wouldn't listen, the stuck-up cow. As for Sam Quiggley: it's two of a kind there, if you ask me. Marriage made in heaven, that'll be, or hell. Well, he's welcome to the little slag!'

'Don't Mum.' I can't bear to hear.

'Don't you "don't" me. I've just about had enough of you. I said to Ian the other night–'

'Don't Mum. Please.'

I hate her. Suddenly I can't bear to look at her Everything about her revolts me. I need to get away.

'Just you stay here, Francis!'

116

I'm opening the front door. I don't bother to reply.

'Where do you think you're going?' She follows me and shouts down the stairwell:

'That's right! Run away, you great big baby, but I'm warning you, Francis, I won't let that girl do this to us. Never. I won't let her drag you down. I'm your mother and don't you forget it. If you think I've gone through everything just to have you throw it all away like this–'

'Well!' Liz Quiggley waddles from her flat. She's smiling. She rests her bulk against the railings, and stretches up her fat, thick throat to let a neat cloud of smoke out into the air. Then she licks her lips.

'Frankie? Who's been a naughty boy then?'

I shrug. She's staring at my lump. Half smiling.

'That's a beauty that is. You're a dark horse, Frankie. I didn't think you had it in you.' She laughs and behind her the balcony rail rattles. It's obvious that she doesn't know what's happened.

I don't know what to say but for the first time ever I wish I wasn't me. I wish I was Sam and that nobody gave a toss about me. Or that I could be me and show everybody what I'm really like.

Down in the car park I begin to run. It jars my head but I don't care. Not now. In fact, I wouldn't mind if I jarred my brain to death.

14

....

Monday afternoon

'My goodness me!' It's Mrs Seagrove. 'You've been in the wars.' She bends over to examine my forehead. 'I expect you'll have a black eye tomorrow, but never mind, luv.' She pats my shoulder. 'How d'you do it? Walk into a lamp-post? I did that a few years back. Or was it one of them meters what they put in Queen's Street? I can't remember now. But I had eyes as black as a panda.'

'It was a table. At school. I fell over it.'

'Dear me. They always say you should put a bit of steak on a lump, don't they?'

'Do they? They only had peas at school. Frozen ones'

'Well, that's it, isn't it? Everything's gone vegetarian these days, with the BS whatever. You can't be too careful, I suppose. Not with kiddies in school. That's why I like a bit of fish, them not having brains.' She's sat beside me in the shelter and is nudging her shopping bag to get it to stand up on its own. A silver fish tail sticks out of a polythene bag. 'It'll be a treat,' she explains, 'for me and Snowy. It's a bit of cod. That's what I do now and again on a nice bright day

118

like this. I come down to the harbour and buy a bit off the boats, if anyone's landed a catch.'

It *is* a nice bright day now she mentions it. Even though it'll soon be Christmas, I can feel the warmth of the sun through the glass shelter. It's lucky because I'm still in those sports things.

In front of us the sea is wide and grey and still. I've been sitting here and thinking about a bit in *Othello*. I'm sure it's at the beginning of Act II. There's been a storm at sea and these gentlemen are waiting around on the shore in Cyprus. They're watching for a sail which will mean the safe arrival of the ship bringing the white lady Desdemona from Venice to her new husband, the black sea captain Othello. When they see the sail they're pleased. They think everything is going to be all right. One of the gentlemen makes this speech about the sea; he says: 'the guttered rocks and congregated sands' have gone specially quiet so that the ship could reach the harbour safely. 'Guttered rocks and congregated sands': I like the sound of it, and I mutter it under my breath. Especially the 'guttered rocks'.

In class we discussed it with Mrs Rushmoor, about how it sometimes seems as though the sea has a mind of its own. Somebody, Vicky, I think, said that after she'd had this flaming row with her mother she came down here to look at the sea. It was a stormy day but she felt much better. She thought it was the afternoon of the spring tides because the waves were dashing up right over the promenade. She said she walked as close as she dared and got soaked through. Afterwards she felt calmer as though the sea had understood her mood and her problems. Some of the class laughed at her but I know what she meant.

That wasn't why I came down here. I came because . . .
that's where the road leads, in the end. It's a long walk. I
only ran a bit, but I could run more, couldn't I, only not
today. But I think I'll try it in the future. I could work up to
it, like a goal. It's made me feel better, sort of calmer. I've
been sitting here thinking about Shakespeare and Emilia. I
haven't thought about the stuff in school. I've thought
about Emilia crossing the Channel from France. That's how
they did it. She and her family were smuggled over in a
container lorry. Yasmina says they paid in gold – and it was
in the papers as well. Anyway, Emilia's father paid loads of
money to these men, traffickers they called them, to
smuggle them out of Romania, and across Europe to
England. Her uncle and his family had done this last year,
and they helped to arrange it. They met up with Emilia and
her lot on the motorway outside Dover. They used the van
we saw in the car park, only somebody must have reported
them.

Emilia had been hidden for several days amongst boxes
and boxes of oranges and lemons from Turkey. It can't have
been much fun. It's bad enough travelling as a normal ferry
passenger in winter. Just imagine being hidden and having
to go deep down into the ship and not knowing what's
happening. It must have been so scary but she says 'no' and
laughs about it. Last week in class she mimed eating oranges
for us. Apparently they broke open one of the crates and ate
a few because they'd finished all their water. I don't suppose
they touched the lemons. It makes my mouth water just to
think about it. Yasmina says that Emilia wanted to leave
Romania and that she's really happy to be here. But I'm not
sure.

120

'I shall poach it,' says Mrs Seagrove, nodding at her bag 'in a spot of milk. Snowy and me like it that way. Then you can see the bones, not like frying. You have to take care with a cat. They can get one stuck somewhere and you'd never know until it's too late.'

I don't mention Snowy's wild feasts in the rubbish behind the Red Lion. She'd only worry more.

'It's nice, isn't it?' I point out to sea. 'It's so . . . peaceful.'

'It is *now*.'

'What do you mean, Mrs Seagrove?'

'Just what I said. It's peaceful now, but in those days, if you came down here you could hear the guns.'

'What guns?'

'In France. In the war. You could hear them all round the South coast. Booming away, especially on an evening, a quiet summer evening. Later, when I was a land girl, I used to sit out when it was fine after work and there'd be skylarks up above singing their hearts out. But from far away you'd hear the boom, boom of the big guns. That sound rolled over the water like a sort of thunder. And I'd sit out with my friend Peg and I'd think about my Ernie. I'd be so glad he wasn't over there amongst those guns, because he didn't like noise. Only I didn't know then did I.'

'Know what?'

'What they'd done to him. Where they'd sent him. Him being a gypsy.'

I don't look at her. She's gripping the handle of the shopping bag as if she's about to leave. She's all worked up. I can see that. I don't know how to stop her.

But I try.

'My grandad, my mum's dad, he was in the war too. In

121

North Africa. He was a Desert Rat. That's what he always said. He was a bit deaf and he said it was because of all that sand in his ears. It took years to come out.' I don't tell her that I believed that story for ages.

'Your grandad was lucky. That's where they should have sent my Ernie, kept him on the land, though I don't know about a desert. It was the *land* he loved. It was what he knew about. That's what Mr Jones wrote to me after. A "wicked waste", that's what he wrote. "A wicked waste of a fine young man".'

She took a great, gulping breath of air and then another. 'My Ernie should have been a sniper. That's what he joined up for. That was his gift and they agreed when he first went before the board. He could hit anything. It's in the eye you know and in the hand. You're born with it. His father was the same. And Ernie'd handled guns since he was knee high. He was what they call a perfect shot. It didn't matter what it was: flying or sitting, running or hiding, he could see it and he could hit it. One shot and it was down. One squeeze, that was what he used to say. And never in anger. I used to go out with him sometimes, because he'd do a bit of poaching, you know, get something for the pot. He'd get so close he could have picked those rabbits out of the grass by their ears.

'I can see him now, with his hat pulled down a bit. He always wore his hat.' She lets a tear trickle down her cheek. 'There was one evening before the war, during the hopping. Me and Peg was waiting for him in the wood like we'd arranged and she thought he wasn't going to come. It was night time but there wasn't a sign of him, not a sound. She wanted to go back, what with the shadows in the wood and us being London girls. And then, there he was. He just stepped out into the clearing. He didn't half make us jump, because we *was* only girls, but he was that quiet. And I liked that. I liked a quiet man after my dad.

'And my Ernie knew those woods like the back of his hand. Every ditch and hedge and every plant and all their seasons. Well, he'd been born there, hadn't he, born in a bender in King's Wood. It was where he belonged, on the land.

'And it's where I would have been with him. If–' She presses an old, folded hankie into each eye. Then brushes down the front of her coat.

'Dear me. It's quite nippy when you sit a bit.' She glances at me sharply and blows her nose. 'You want to take care, young man! You could catch a cold with no coat.'

I nod and lick my lips. I can taste the salt. She's right. It is cold. It is winter but I can almost see that autumn wood, King's Wood, on the edge of the hop fields. The two of them are standing close together. The friend, Peg, is a little way off, looking the other way. He's reaching over, stroking her hair back from her face, and their feet are covered over by the thickly fallen leaves.

'He won all the prizes, you know, for shooting. Mr Jones said that they were very proud of him in the regiment; they'd never seen anything like it. Of course I didn't know that then, because Ernie didn't write. He'd never learnt. Not that he didn't want to. And I'd promised to teach him when he got back. It was all we talked about: what we'd do when he got back

'Only they didn't want him to be a marksman, did they? Not those officers in the army. Oh dear me no! Couldn't trust a *gypsy*, they said. Not with a gun. "You never know which way they'll point it." That's what they said. I'll never forget him telling me that later. He was that angry. It was his last leave before he went and it was the only time I'd ever seen him lose his temper, whereas my dad lost his every Friday night and in between too. "Never trust a gypsy", those were the officer's very words. Just like little Hitlers, all over again.'

'So . . . so what happened, Mrs Seagrove?'

'Sent him overseas, didn't they? Mr Jones pleaded for him, took up his case and that, because he was educated, for all he was a tallyman, but it did no good. They shut him up in a troopship with thousands of other poor devils and sent him out to the Far East, or tried to.'

'Tried to?'

'Well, he didn't get there, did he? I mean he wouldn't, would he? It was the one thing he was afraid of: the sea. Lots of gypsies are. They don't like to go on the sea. Not if they can possibly avoid it. He told them that, said he couldn't, said he'd do *anything* but that, but they didn't listen. They knew best, didn't they? Even though they was as ignorant as pigs, that's what Mr Jones told me later. As ignorant as pigs and even then he reckoned that was doing an injustice to pigs.

'Well, he jumped ship, didn't he, at the first port, but the military police caught him and brought him back in irons. Beat him within an inch of his life and then put him back on board. Shut him away deep down in the hold with those great engines turning and turning night and day. Him, who'd never had a key turned on him, never been shut away from the stars in the sky.'

124

'And?'

'Goodness me! Look at the time. I've got to be getting back.'

But I know there will be more. Later.

'Mrs Seagrove, can I ask you something?'

'Don't you think you've asked enough? Keeping an old woman like me out in the cold. You young people, you–'

'Has there ever been a fire in Poet's Rise?'

'A fire?' She turns back.

'Yes. In one of the blocks.'

'No. Not that I can remember and I've been here since '73, though Mrs Turner's chip pan caught alight once. But that was years and years ago. You wasn't even born then, I daresay, and her son put it out with a bit of carpet which is better than water. And there was a car, wasn't there, back in the summer. But not a *house* fire. Not as I remember. Why?'

'It's just that somebody, a teacher, I think, drew this picture at school. It showed a fire, in Poet's Rise.'

'Well,' she snaps, 'there hasn't been one yet, but with your friends the Quiggleys so busy and important these days, you never know. Do you?'

She's watching me closely.

'The Quiggleys aren't my friends. None of them.'

'Oh no?'

'No!'

'Well, it's not what I've heard. Or seen, because I keep my eye on things. And I've heard what your mother and Liz Quiggley have to say. I read it in the papers. And it's disgusting. There's enough hate and anger being breathed about in Poet's Rise to make the whole estate go up in flames. It won't need no chip pan. "Space not race" – what sort of disgusting rubbish is that? Well, I'll tell you. It's Hitler's sort, what we saw off all those years ago. Only it's back, isn't it! And I'm surprised at your mother. I really am. I'm sorry luv, but it's got to be said.'

'I know. I'm sorry too.' Suddenly, impossibly, I think I'm going to cry, except that I can't. Not at my age and especially when nothing has happened.

'She never used to be like this. Honestly, Mrs Seagrove. I hate it. All of it. And I hate her. I hate her, even though she's my mum.'

I'm waiting for her to protest, to say that I mustn't talk about June like that, but she doesn't. She tucks a little scarf back into the collar of her coat and shakes the fish down into the bag.

'Well,' she says, quite cheerfully, 'I've said what I think and Snowy will be waiting. I'll have to take the bus, you kept me so long. How about you?'

'I'm . . . I'm going to finish my run.' I haven't any money but I'm not telling her that. She might offer to pay. I jog up and down on the spot.

'Well, if you're sure. But you watch where you're going this time. No more running into tables!'

126

15

....

Monday night

Who says running keeps you warm? I'm frozen now and too cold to stay out any longer. My toes are dead. If I get pneumonia or hypothermia they'll rush me to hospital, won't they? But then I could refuse to see Mum. The doctors would have to turn her away. She'd cry and plead and even claim it's her right to see me, I bet; but it won't do any good. They'd still shake their heads. 'Later perhaps,' they'd say, 'when he's stronger.'

My teeth are chattering. My nose is running and I haven't got a tissue. I wipe it on my sleeve. Nobody's looking but I was quick.

Mum refuses to turn round when I go into the kitchen. I suspect things are bad even before I notice her single dish on the table. The back of her neck is red and blotchy. She's stirring soup; stirring determinedly and hunched up over the stove as though she's cold too. Toast pops up. She butters it, then tips the soup out too quickly. It slops over the edge. It's tomato, naturally. I always suspected it was *her* favourite, all along.

She's sitting with her back to me and I'm so mad. So cold

and so mad. She just sits there, crunching toast. No wonder she and my grandma fell out. I've never thought of it like this before, but Mum's impossible. Absolutely impossible. Even Liz Quiggley would have said *some*thing. '–ff off' maybe, but that's better than silence, and the sound of her teeth grinding down the toast.

I run the bath, climb in and submerge myself. Or some of me. I top it up again and again, trying to get warm. I wallow in it, knowing that she's next door and dying to bang on the wall to tell me to pack it in and stop wasting hot water. But nothing happens. She doesn't make a sound – doesn't dare, most likely. She must know that she's wrong and that I've got her sussed.

When I finally climb out it's still only just after seven. Time's never gone so slowly. I'm as tired as if it's way past midnight. And hungry. I'm absolutely starving, to tell the truth.

Even Snowy is getting a fish tea this evening, and poached in milk. I picture them sitting down together afterwards. They'll snuggle up on the sofa with that pink knitted thing around them both. The desperate little bar will be blazing away but hardly shifting the cold at all. I expect the box of photos is still out. She'll reach over and take one out; her thumb will rub the dust from his face, rub slowly back and forth, as she remembers things.

Here Mum's got the telly on. It's soaps. I creep past the door. The fridge is almost empty. I knew it. There's not even an egg. She's taken the last slices of bread, just leaving me bits of crust. That's *so* selfish. It was never like this before. She used to hand over a list and some money when she went to the salon and I'd do the shopping on the way home from school. The fridge was never empty then.

If Mrs Seagrove was *my* gran, I could have nipped down there, couldn't I? She'd have looked after me. Proper grandparents do: look at Mrs Morris and Katy. They even went on holiday together.

I can't help remembering that somewhere out there my *own* grandmother is probably sitting in front of her telly. And might be thinking about me. I bet she dreams of me too, and always listens for an unfamiliar knock, my knock, on her door. Do you know, in all these years I've never had a real idea of what my grandmother would look like. I can't picture her, except for the checked dress and Mum's pop eyes. It's odd, too, that my grandad never mentioned her when he visited us. You'd expect him to, wouldn't you? She was his wife. But he never did. Now I think I know why: it's because of Mum. He didn't want to annoy her. He knew how impossible she is, how unforgiving, and he didn't want any more trouble.

It's as if I've been living with a stranger all these years; almost as if I've been adopted and only just found out. It's as if I don't really belong in this home at all. And who says my grandma is a rubbish sort of person, apart from Mum? Nobody, actually. So maybe she isn't. Maybe she's just different. Why should I believe Mum now? My grandma could be . . . anybody. She could be absolutely brilliant and not like Mum at all. She could be like . . . Mrs Morris, couldn't she, sort of educated and . . . thoughtful. Like . . . even like this Alicia, Alicia Fontwell, who sent me that book.

All this time when Mum's struggled so hard to bring me up, I thought she was a real heroine. You know the scene: young single mother battles on to bring up only son who makes good. Our life was a play and we were both in it, acting our roles, her and me, and now it doesn't seem real at all. Maybe there was another plot all along, another house where we could have been, a *real* home, waiting for us somewhere. Only Mum wouldn't have it. She was too proud or too pigheaded to accept any help. She's prevented me having that life just like she's prevented me from having a grandma.

It could be like that, couldn't it? It would explain loads. It would explain why I'm so different from Mum, why I want to be an actor or a writer, or even a film maker. Mum calls these 'arty farty' jobs and says they're not real jobs at all. I don't agree. I never have and that might be because I'm like this grandma: a chip off the old block, as people say.

And Dad? *My* dad? He's another thing we've never talked about. Not really. She's always discussed her *other* men, talked endlessly about them. And her. Lots of it I never wanted to hear, though at the time I did, in a way, but she never talked about *my* dad. She just said that he cleared off as soon as he knew she was pregnant. I've always thought that was such a lousy thing to do but I never asked for details. No one wants to hear that their father's a total loss, do they? And she never seemed particularly upset about it. I don't think she cared. So she couldn't have loved him, could she? Not . . . true love? Not when you compare her with Mrs Seagrove, who's still in love, after all these years. There's no box of photos in our flat. I've always assumed that he didn't love her either. Or me. I've always believed that he never ever saw me.

Now, I'm not sure. Maybe he did. Maybe he left because of Mum and the way she is. Maybe he never noticed until too late, how impossible she is. How she's a different person inside. I think he stopped loving her when he discovered that she was two-faced, but then it was too late.

Suddenly I remember what Iago says about women, about how tricky they are. I take the bag of crusts and go back into my room. *Othello* is on my bed. I leaf through, dropping crumbs. It's early on, yes, here it is:

Come on, come on; you are pictures out doors,
Bells in your parlours, wildcats in your kitchens,
Saints in your injuries; devils being offended,
Players in your housewifery, and housewives in your beds!

It's true. It really is. When we read it in class all the girls were furious. They said it was 'anti-women', but they're just mad feminists. Everything's stupid girl power with them. Iago's not anti-woman. He's just describing someone exactly like my mum; she's 'a saint in her injuries'. Oh yes! And she's false.

'Francis–'

'Mum!' She's at my door and has made me jump. I put an arm over Shakespeare as if it's a dirty mag.

'Francis? We've got to talk.' Her face is so swollen. Her eyes lost in tears. She's not just froggy. She's a toad and she disgusts me too. Anyway, I can't see what she's got to cry about. I'm the one who got hurt today.

'OK. Talk! Talk all you like. But do you know what? This isn't the Church Hall. And I don't have to listen.'

She's staring at me, more pop-eyed than ever. I'm pretty shocked too. I didn't plan those words. They just . . . came. But I'm pleased. Her lips are trembling.

'Don't do this, Francis. You've got to listen to me. I'm your *mother*. I care about you.'

'Oh yes?'

'Yes! And whatever you think, I *do* know what's for the best. And this girl isn't it. She'll move, Frankie. They're gypsies, for crying out loud! That's what gypsies do, in case you hadn't noticed. They move on. They make a mess and then they move out leaving the rest of us to clear up their stink. You can't trust them, even if you want to. Nobody can. She'll break your heart and then she'll leave you–'

'I don't care. At least I've got a heart to break. At least I know how to love someone!'

'Love? You call *this* "love"? Then you're even more stupid than I thought. You don't know what you're talking about. "Love" indeed!'

'You don't know a thing about it.' I speak quietly, almost patiently, and that gets her going even more.

'Love,' she snorts. 'You've never even taken her out! Have you?'

I stop myself answering. I turn my back on her, open up old *Othello* again and pretend to read.

'Have you, Frankie?'

I turn another page and smile to myself. So she has to back off. It feels like victory, only nobody is cheering.

I don't go to school the next day. Mum doesn't call me so I don't bother. I turn over and listen for her to go. Then I doze until nearly two. I plan to dream about Emilia. And try, but it's no good. When I finally wake I'm too hot and bursting for a pee.

Then I hear something. That's pretty odd but it sounds like someone in the bathroom. It's probably a cat or the wind, but I've got to open the door. I can't wait.

'Sorry! I didn't realize–'

'That's all right,' Lucy snatches at a towel. She turns towards me, still smiling the end of a smile that she must have begun before. She's been standing in the bath, inspecting herself in the mirror. There's a patch rubbed clear on the steamy glass but the water is already trickling down again. Her face is bright pink; so are her thin little legs and her bum where the towel has slipped.

'Your Mum said I could,' she giggles.

The water must have been boiling. She looks more cooked than washed. Now she pushes her fringe back and chews on the corner of the striped towel. My towel, actually, but I suppose it was the first to hand.

'Your mum said a hot bath would help. Dad thinks I'm getting flu. He sent me home from school and when I saw your mum in the street, she told me to come here. And gave me her key. She didn't think I should go all that way on the bus to our house. Not with a temperature. She said "have a bath and a rest". She's so kind, your mum, isn't she Frankie? I really like her.'

'She's a toad—'

'Ooh! Aren't you awful! But I'll go away if you mind. Do you mind? Frankie? I'll get dressed and go straightaway. It's no trouble. I didn't know you were still here. Your mum never said, so I thought you were in school. Have you got flu too? Are you ill, Frankie?'

'No. I just didn't fancy school today. That's all.'

'You boys! Aren't you awful! You just don't care, do you Frankie? I wouldn't dare wag school.' She lifts the towel up a bit and tries to tuck it round.

'But I'm ever so glad you *are* here, Frankie. Honestly. I

133

don't like being on my own. I'm not very brave, not on my own, not like you, Frankie. Don't you ever get scared?'

'Me? No way!'

'Wow! I wish I was like that. Like you.'

She looks like a prawn, so pink and bent over, clutching my towel. What does she think I'm going to do? Grab it back? No way: dream on, Lucy! No thank you very much! And with her belly button still not healed, the sight of her makes me want to puke. She's a mess.

She grins more widely and shrugs her skinny little shoulders. I grin too. After all, what else is there to do? Except have a pee.

Next day in school I learn that I've missed a real sensation. Emilia's father turned up in the middle of the second lesson. He wanted to take her away. He came with his brother and they caused such a commotion barging into classrooms looking for her that the police were called. Then Social Services. And do you know what? Emilia wouldn't go with them! She clung to Yasmina and shouted 'No! No! No!' and the police couldn't do anything. They hadn't got the right and didn't want to either when they saw how upset she was.

Social Services found a translator who knows a bit of her language and it turns out that Emilia's been longing to go to school all her life, that she's never had a chance before. Now it's happened she's really happy and wants to stay, only her parents aren't keen. They never wanted her to go to school and are really upset that it's boys and girls mixed. They hadn't realized it would be like that and they don't think it's right. But Emilia does. And apparently she said this to her father in the Axe's office and he got up and left. He and

134

his brother just walked out. Then she burst into tears. Everyone's talking about it.

I'm so mad that I missed it. If I'd been there I could have helped. I could have told them what I'd seen that very first evening when she only had flip-flops on in all that rain and her little brother was pushing her about. I knew she wasn't like the others. Not really.

'So where's she now?' I ask Yasmina and Vicky, because Emilia's not in the classroom.

'With Mrs Morris. She's going to stay there for a bit.' Then I remember: Mrs Morris takes kids in. She's done it before when someone has had a row at home and been thrown out. It's like fostering I think. Last year people say that one of the sixth form girls had a baby and took it to Mrs Morris for a bit, when her own parents wouldn't have them home.

'Will she be back tomorrow?' I ask.

'I dunno. I think so, though. I think someone said they were going to get her some proper clothes. Uniform and stuff. It's brilliant of Mrs Morris, isn't it? It's so–'

Yasmina stops and gives me a look.

'Only I don't suppose you think like that, do you, Frankie?'

'What do you mean? Of *course* I do! Of *course* I think it's brilliant. Honestly, Yasmina, everybody's got it wrong about me. *I'm* not part of Mum's campaign. It's nothing to do with me. I don't agree with it anyway. And I'm sick of being blamed for her ideas. So you can tell everybody that, Yasmina. My mum is just . . . pathetic. Really pathetic. I'm Emilia's friend. I always have been. After all, I got to know her before any of you!'

16

....

Saturday 19 December

It's only four-thirty pm and almost dark. Nowadays I put the light on as soon as I step into the flat. It's so gloomy. The last few days have skidded by in a grey rush, like tube trains underground; they've followed each other with only a cold, grey wind in between. It's always like this before Christmas, even though it's not a big deal at all, especially for people like Mum and me, with no real family. But that doesn't stop it being a rush: a rush and fuss about nothing at all, just like Arshad said. And it's about as much fun as a wet nappy.

It's not as if Mum and I are struggling to cope with twenty-seven invading relations, a turkey the size of Wales and carol singers stamping the snow off their boots and expecting home-made mince pies and steaming punch. Round here it's not like that. It's a telly and frozen chicken kind of Christmas in Poet's Rise, with a cheap toy from the market if you're a kid and socks if you're not.

Actually I'm glad I'm no longer a kid. I don't expect anything now, so I'm not disappointed. But I used to be. I used to think I'd die of disappointment. One year I really thought she was going to give me a red mountain bike! God, was I miserable. I'd opened everything in less than a minute and that was that: no bikes under our mangy tree.

Mum enjoys Christmas – but then I've always given her what she wanted, which is smellies, like bubble baths and special soaps. Every year she is surprised how I remember and how I always pick out her favourites. But I'm good at that sort of thing. The trouble is she isn't. She's never got me what I really wanted and I'm no good at pretending to be pleased. Faking it, as it were. I suppose Christmas was a bit more fun when my grandad came round, but that never happened until Boxing Day. The twenty-fifth was always just her and me, with nothing to do except nibble through stacks and stacks of food like a pair of mad hamsters.

Last year she was just getting to know Ian. They'd met at a school do – the carol service, I think, or maybe the Christmas charity disco. Then he sent her a Christmas card. I knew at once that this was something special. The card itself was different: a star made out of twisted grass and stuck on green paper. We never get cards like that. Ours are always very cheap and very, very Christmassy. Mum kept reading it again and again; she kept saying 'how *nice* of him! Francis, isn't that *nice*?' All it said was 'Happy Christmas from Ian and Lucy Bresslaw'. To begin with I thought 'Lucy' was his wife. I mean, that's the most likely thing, isn't it?

I didn't actually meet Lucy until New Year's Eve. Of course by then I knew she was Ian's daughter. Ian and Mum were going out to a party and they'd arranged for Lucy to stay at ours and for me to babysit. I didn't mind at all. In fact, when I first saw her I thought what a sweet little kid she was and even thought stuff about dear little kid sisters. She was *so* good. She did whatever I told her and straightaway.

And she smiled at me all the time from under her fringe. We played hide-and-seek for a bit, which was unfair, in a way, because she'd never been in the flat before and didn't know any of the places. She said she didn't mind. I made her a snack and she was very impressed and told me that Ian couldn't cook as well and then we watched a video. It was one of Mum's. She'd hidden it but I'd seen her. It was, well, quite adult and after a bit I wished I hadn't got it out, but I couldn't say that, could I, to Lucy. I couldn't just switch it off, so we watched to the end. I made Lucy promise not to tell. She promised at once and didn't ask for anything in return.

Now, I think it was really sneaky of Ian and Mum. They exploited me totally. And Lucy. They never even asked us what we wanted to do on New Year's Eve.

There's another charity disco this year. Pupils can go from our year upwards if they're with family or grown-up friends. I'd thought about it – well, more than thought, actually. At half-term I'd even decided to give a hint to Ian, but it won't be happening now. Mum would never consider it because this year's charity is gypsy communities around the world! Mrs Morris has put up an exhibition about them.

I saw a poster about it this morning. The art department must have done it. They usually do. Lots of the girls are going. They've been talking about it all week. It's supposed to be quite special, like the high school proms they have in America. You can wear black tie if you want to, or 'ethnic dress'. That's what the ticket said. Arshad showed us his. I was so surprised that he's going with his mum and dad. And a bit jealous, if I'm honest. I've never been to anything like that. At least it would have been a laugh.

Well, it wouldn't, actually. Not with the mood Mum's in. And Paris obviously isn't happening either. Ian's hardly been round at all recently. Lucy comes round quite often and she and Mum have got really pally. Mum did her hair the other night. Ian's very busy, or so they said. And that's about all Mum has said to me: just the odd word here or there.

It's as though everything is shutting down around me. I can't believe that it's only two or three weeks since that morning when Emilia came into school. But I suppose it's winter. Everything stops. I haven't seen Mrs Seagrove for ages. That's the winter too: it's almost dark when I get in and then I go straight to my room. I finished *Othello* last week and I've started on *Romeo and Juliet*. I told Mrs Rushmore and she was so impressed. I still haven't got that video. I haven't been in the library: like I said, it's Christmas and there's stuff to do.

'Francis?' Mum is outside my door. She doesn't barge in now.

'When Lucy comes, tell her to wait. I've got to go out now, but I'll be back.'

'Right.'

'And you could make her something to eat, couldn't you, if she wanted it?'

'Right.'

'I won't be late–'

'Whatever!'

People were talking about Mrs Morris's exhibition today. I'd like to go. I *am* interested, but I feel awkward after the Sam thing. I'm uncomfortable thinking about it and the way she stepped straight over me, just as if I wasn't important. She shouldn't have taken sides like that, especially after I've spent so long in her library, helping out. She should understand, because other teachers do.

The Axe did. I've got to hand it to old Chester. She's tough but she's fair. She said hello to me yesterday, using my name. 'Hi Francis,' she snapped as she strode down the corridor, 'how's the running?' I was surprised she remembered. We'd hardly mentioned it during that talk. When she'd finally leant back in a chair and groaned, she told me that I was a fool: a clumsy, blundering fool. Yes, she groaned again, she *did* believe me. Just. She understood that I'd never meant to do anything other than help Emilia, but I'd gone the wrong way about it. She said I'd done harm but that it wasn't too late. 'What else do you do, Francis?' she had snarled, 'when you're not scaring girls by grabbing their wrists and smashing up the art room?' She wasn't laughing at me. Not really. It was worse than that. It was more like she pitied me. I didn't know what to say. I wasn't even sure if she was asking a question.

'Well?' Her voice was like a fist in my ear.

'I . . . run . . . a bit.' That's all I said. But she'd remembered, hadn't she? And looked back at me in the corridor. She spun right round, her arms full of papers, her rough red hair all over the place.

'Well?' she barked.

'I'm going this evening . . . Miss Chester . . . I think.'

'I think you'd better,' she said and went on.

It's drizzling outside. The car park and the pavements are shining with black grease. It's not the evening for a run, but it's not the evening for anything else either. And Lucy's coming. She and Mum will clog up the whole flat with their idiotic laughter and their meaningful looks.

I change into my running gear. Half way down the stairs and going fast I crash into Lucy. Literally.

'God I'm sorry. I didn't see you. Honestly.' I've knocked her into the wall.

'That's all right, Frankie.'

'Are you hurt?'

'No!' But she's looking at the back of her hand. Her knuckles are grazed. Her hand must have banged against the concrete.

'It's nothing!' she says.

'I'm sorry.' I feel bad about it. I don't like her but I didn't mean to hurt her. Not like that.

'It's all right!' she says shrilly. There's a bright dab of blood. The skin around is mottled pink and blue. She lifts her hand slowly to her mouth and touches her tongue on to the spot, and stares at me from under her fringe. She's holding out her fist, trembling.

'You could kiss it better then, couldn't you, Frankie? If you're so sorry . . . '

It's like a claw, a tiny bird's claw. Sometimes you see them dead in the gutter. Their claws are curled over and stiff and the skin is roughened, pink and grey.

I kiss it. I mean – so what? Poor kid, poor little, stupid little Lucy.

Then I begin my run. I don't see them until it's too late to stop. Suddenly I'm pounding out of Magnolia Drive and straight into them.

17

....

Saturday night

I'd zipped past the Red Lion and along the High Street. After
that I'd slowed down. I didn't want to stop completely in
case someone was watching. They might think I was a fat,
out of condition slob, which I'm not, so I just kept going.
Barry always goes on about getting a second wind and
breaking through pain barriers. I've never believed him. I've
always given up when I began gasping for breath, but not
today. Today I'm still running. I'm not going fast and my
chest hurts as I draw in breaths that aren't enough, but I'm
still moving. Just.

I can feel the sweat running down my back and between
my legs and that's gross. It's wet and cold on my face as
well, even though my skin's on fire. I bet I'm more than
pink. I'm probably purple. Barry nags us about our arms, so
I'm working those too. It makes a difference and I'm
covering ground again as I burst out of Magnolia Drive
and slap bang into the back of this crowd. Only I didn't
realize it was a crowd. I thought it was a jam of Christmas
shoppers or something.

'Hey! Hold on!' A policewoman in a luminous jacket

sticks out her arm. 'You can't go through there! You'll have to wait.'

'I only want–'

'I said "wait", didn't I?'

She's slightly smaller than me despite her helmet and the yellow luminous thing, but she looks very determined. I step back. Then I see the placards. And Liz Quiggley. She's perching on a concrete flower trough outside the Council Building. It's a good job it's winter: there are no helpless flowers in it waiting to be trampled on, only a dying sort of fir thing. She's straddling it, trying to keep her balance on the narrow concrete edge. She's such a silly old cow! It's hilarious. If I wasn't alone I'd have laughed, but you need someone to join in if you're going to crack up in public.

Liz is having serious trouble raising her placard and staying upright. Her huge boobs, and that whacking chunk of wood with 'no gyppos here!!' painted on in dribbled black letters, keep tipping her forward again so that her bum sticks up in the air. It looks like a bit of sawn-off door – the placard, that is – not her bum. Not quite.

There's a large group of people around her and more on the Council steps. I can pick out two of her sons, Keith and Alan, and several others from the Poet's Rise Estate. That's one of Mrs Seagrove's neighbours, Ken. He's a bus driver. And that big guy is Trevor Jackson. He's Vicky Jackson's cousin or stepbrother or something. He runs the gym in the High Street. Those beefy blokes with him must be body-builders. They are enormous but they look as if their necks are slowly swallowing up their heads. I hope that runners don't suffer from anything nasty like that.

And I hope Mum isn't here. Please, let her be somewhere

143

else. I'd completely forgotten about her when I was pounding along just now. Stuck here like this I've remembered and it makes me sick. I glance around nervously; I bet she is around and stupidly mixed up with this lot. Trevor Jackson is handing out leaflets. His armband says 'official march steward' and he's looking pretty pleased with himself. Actually, now I can see that there are more people watching the protest than are taking part in it. I've seen Arshad's parents and several people from school and Miss Fisher from the doctors'. They're all watching. Just for a minute I think I catch sight of Mrs Seagrove, but I'm not sure. Most of the people out this evening are barely giving the demonstration a second glance. They're deep into their Christmas shopping. I've noticed a young couple in the crowd. They're walking arm in arm and they're carrying lots of bags. I feel odd, watching them, jealous almost. I've never done anything like that, ever, not even with a sister or a cousin or – anybody. Never. Not yet.

Trevor is approaching me smiling. His mouth is open, so I suppose it's a smile, anyway. But he couldn't possibly recognize me, could he? I'm not friends with Vicky, so he must know that he and I are strangers. I look away.

'Here you are folks! Read all about it. Read what we have to say. Read what the people really think about gypsies . . . '

I'm studying my feet. I'm not part of this. I just took a wrong turn. That's all.

'Thanks, mate!' The thin, scruffy man beside me holds his hand out for one of the leaflets. What a creep. Or a wino, because I'm sure that's what he is. In fact, I've seen him around here somewhere. He could be one of those old guys who stagger out of the alley behind the Red Lion. Only he isn't very old: just very drunk.

'Over here then, mate,' he says thickly, still holding his hand out. He's swaying from left to right but his bright blue eyes are clear. He'll only use the leaflets for loo-roll or roll-ups. That's what the homeless do.

Trevor is grinning. He hands over a stack and the wino starts to pass them out in wads to people around him. He even tries to give some to me, but I shake my head. I'm not getting involved. No way. He shrugs, turns from me and begins to talk to no one in particular.

'Hey! You there!' He sways into an open space. People look away.

'Friends–' Now they're looking. Liz looks too. She totters and almost drops her placard.

'Mr Muscle,' the wino shouts, 'a minute of your valuable time!' Trevor lumbers over.

'What's up mate?' Trev's hands rest appreciatively on his six-pack.

'Here,' laughs the wino, 'this is for you!' Quick as a flash he's crumpled a leaflet into a ball. 'This is what I think about you people and this is what I think of what you say!' He flings the ball straight at Trevor's face. Trev ducks. Then he narrows his eyes and rolls his small head about on the top of his vast neck.

Suddenly he's being pelted from all sides. Paper balls are whizzing through the air before dropping to their deaths on the pavement below. Trevor is trying to fend them off. He sticks up hands like dinner plates, but it's no good. He shuts his mouth. He has changed his mind.

He's going to get this wino. He's going to teach him a

lesson. People are backing away. They fan out like ash blown from an ember at the base of a fire. The policewoman steps forward. Her hand is on the baton at her side. The wino steadies himself.

'Come on then, my beauty,' he whispers.

Then, from nowhere at all, Sam Quiggley darts from the crowd and gets between. He grabs hold of Trevor but is flung off like a wet glove. The policewoman raises her baton above him but somehow Sam cringes from her grasp. The crowd pushes away further and faster and somewhere someone stumbles and falls. They'd run if they could, but they can't. There are too many other people around so they scatter as best they can. They are opening up an arena so that Trevor can get at his prey.

'Come on, come on then, my beauty.' The wino puts up his fists. He bends his dirty neck and tucks in his chin.

'Come on, come on,' he chants, hopping up and down on broken shoes, as though the hunter needed to be tempted at all. 'Come on, you filthy, rotten scum!'

The policewoman is talking into her radio. I can hear her fear. She's not so determined now. Liz has dropped her placard. She staggers from the trough and yells encouragement as Trevor Jackson swings his fist into the wino's face. And misses, because Sam is on him again. He's bitten him on the hand. Trevor stares at the bite and at Sam in puzzled disbelief. Then he roars. He fills the space with such a noise that you'd think Sam had bitten his hand clean off.

Sam is circling around, but he won't get away. His two stepbrothers and Liz are closing in behind. Sam spits. He wipes his mouth, then spits again. And just before Trevor Jackson kicks him to the ground he screams:

146

'You leave my dad alone. All of you. You rotten bullies, you . . . ' He curls up as his stepbrothers and Trevor begin to kick. I don't know if anyone else heard and whether they care if they did. The police are everywhere now and the crowd is only interested in getting away. I am as well. Another fight has broken out and I've lost sight of Sam. I don't know where to go or what to do. Somewhere glass breaks and people are running down the street. I still haven't seen Sam or that man he called his dad. I haven't even seen Liz. Nor Mum – which is a good sign, surely. Maybe she didn't even come. Maybe she's started to listen to Ian.

'Frankie!'

'Mum!' For one second I think we're going to fling our arms around each other, only we don't. She steps away from me and lets out a deep breath.

'What about Lucy?' Her voice is irritable as if she's had to ask what time it is.

'Lucy?' I don't follow this. 'What about Lucy?'

'You don't mean you've left her all on her own so that you could come and play the fool with that lot?' She nods towards the remnants of the group opposing the march.

'Honestly, Frankie. You might show me a bit of loyalty.'

'*Loyalty*? Play the fool? For chrissake Mum–'

'Now don't you swear at me, Frankie!'

I look at her closely. I stare into her sour little froggy face and I can't imagine how anyone ever loved this woman who is so stupid and so blind, because *I* don't love her. Not now. Not after this.

'Frankie?'

I turn away.

'Frankie!'

People talk about the blind leading the blind, don't they?

'Frankie . . . '

And that's *us*, isn't it? That's Mum and Liz. And me too, if I'm honest.

Halfway along Magnolia Drive someone else says my name. Whispers it, but I hear and stop. It's a street of curtained windows and parked cars with a dark deserted church at the end. Sam steps from behind a parked van. He's bent over, holding his side. That must be where his stepbrothers and Trev Jackson put the boot in.

'You all right?'

Sam nods. I don't know what to say either so we begin to walk back in silence. It's OK. It's not awkward. It's how we usually walk, only this time I have to slow down. Sam's limping. I glance at him under a streetlight. Now that I know, it's obvious that he's that man's son. They're so similar in build: so slight, so thin, so clearly father and son, even before you've noticed their bright blue eyes. But I don't say anything. I'm trying to stop my teeth chattering, it's that cold. I shouldn't be sauntering along without a jacket on a night like this. It's taking us forever to reach the High Street. Sam isn't complaining. I suppose he's used to it – like Emilia in bare feet in all that rain. And now I think about it, I can't remember her complaining about anything. You'd expect she would, because people are saying that gypsy families like hers were chased out of their homes and beaten up. But she never grumbles.

'Sam . . . ?'

He doesn't answer, just throws up violently. I don't know what to do. He's leaning against the wall. Now he's clutching it and I hear his fingernails scrape down the brick. He's only just staying upright, resting his cheek on his arm. His bright blue eyes are closed. I get one arm under him. It's awkward but I manage. We stagger about twenty yards. Ten more, and I'm as good as carrying him. His feet drag along the pavement. Then he's sick again, over both our shoes. A couple turn to watch. As we stumble by one mutters about 'kids today'! I want to tell her, tell everyone that Sam isn't drunk. He's hurt. Some filthy brutes kicked him in the ribs. That's what's the matter. And he needs help. And I do too.

I sort of pick him up. It's like you would a little kid. He's sprawled in my arms. His head is lolling back and his feet are dangling. He's sick again, but not so much, just a dribble really. Then I see the dreadful streak of bright red blood, like a thread, across his throat and chin.

As I push open the door to the Red Lion, Barry leaps to his feet and races towards me. He takes Sam gently from my arms and lays him down on the floor. He knows what to do. Later, when we're standing around watching the ambulance men get to work, Barry pulls off his sweater and puts it around me.

'He'll be OK,' he says and pats my arm. 'I'm sure he'll be OK.'

I'm nodding, but the rotten thing is, until Barry said that I never even thought that Sam might not be OK. And I never asked him about his father, or Emilia, or anything at all.

18

....

Almost midnight

I hear Mum's voice from a floor down. So she's back. She must have left them to it. It isn't that she's shouting exactly, but her voice is so shrill and so sharp it drills through the concrete. It's echoing in the stairwell. Barry must be able to hear it too, but he doesn't mention it. We're climbing the stairs in silence now, but we talked on the way back. It was about running, mainly. He said that I might be good over long distances, if I wanted to. Though I might not have speed, I'd got 'stamina'. It's decent of him, especially after what he said in the school changing rooms the other week. He could be trying to make it up to me, because I'm upset about Sam.

I *am* upset. And scared. The paramedic fixed up a drip even before they put Sam in the ambulance. That can't be good, can it? The police were searching for Liz to take her to the hospital. I wanted to go too, but they said not yet. I *will* go. They can't stop me. I don't see why they were so keen to take Liz. It was her precious sons, his stepbrothers, who gave Sam that kicking! Outside our front door I take off Barry's sweater. While I'm struggling out of it I hear Ian quite clearly. He must be just on the other side.

'June,' he's saying, 'I can't do this any longer. I'm sorry. I can't go on: either you pack in this campaign, or it's the end, the end of you and me. I can't take it, June, not any more. You know I've never agreed with you about space not race, but this – this is too much.'

She isn't replying, or if she does, we can't hear. I'm glad the sweater is hiding my face.

'This is going to end badly, June,' he continues. 'All this anger and hatred washing around this estate, around you, June.'

'Go on then, Ian. Go!' That's Mum. She's screaming at him. 'Clear off then, Ian. Run back to your precious Alicia and all your arty farty friends. I'm not stopping you. Go and stick your posh head in your posh sand! Go on then!'

There's another silence. Ridiculously I find myself hoping that Mum will relent and that Ian will stay.

'Still here?' she mocks. 'Well, let me tell you that this is the *real* world. The *real* world's here, in Poet's Rise. We call a spade a spade and you may not like that, but you can't change it. So if you're afraid, Ian, you'd better get out. Hadn't you?'

Inside the house one of them puts a hand on the lock.

'Look here, Frankie.' Barry grabs the sweater off me. 'Don't worry about Sam. I'll go there now. I'll let you know.' He can't wait to escape. I don't blame him. I only wish I could. Before either of us can make a move, the door bursts open and Ian crashes out with a heap of his stuff piled up in a sagging cardboard box. Mum is on the step still in her outdoor clothes. She can't have been back long. Maybe she saw what happened to Sam.

The four of us stare at each other. It's an embarrassing,

ugly moment like a massive spot oozing in public and I just want to die. Eventually Barry mutters something to Mum about an accident and how he thought he'd better see me home. Safely. It makes me cringe. What a 'home'! I bet that's what he's thinking. Maybe the same thought has struck Mum because as soon as Barry mentions the accident and Sam, she leaps on me. She flings her arms around me like a devoted mother and bursts into tears. Real, wet tears. She's sniffing against my ear. I give her a shove and get her off me, but she doesn't let go completely. I can still feel her.

'Well, go on then.' She snarls across me at Ian and includes Barry in her scowl. She's never liked him. 'Clear off, the both of you! I don't need people like you telling me how to run my life. I've got my *son*, haven't I? *He'll* stand by me, won't you Frankie, eh?'

I don't say anything until they've gone. We're standing close. She's gripping my arm so tightly, her nails are digging in. When they've disappeared I jerk free. She's breathing rapidly, watching my face with her hands now clasped beneath her chin.

'Soup?' she asks faintly. When I don't reply she sniffs back tears, rubs her bulging brimming eyes and even smiles. 'Toast?'

I don't believe this is happening.

'Tomato? Or something else? To warm you up?'

I just can't believe she's doing this, but I should have known, shouldn't I? Iago had warned me: 'players in your housewifery'. That's her. And this game stinks of the good housewife.

I follow her into the kitchen and sit down at the table. I'm exhausted. My feet ache after running. I undo the laces and ease my trainers off. She's looking in the fridge, wiping her eyes, filling the kettle. In another minute she'll be humming a tune.

'I don't want anything to eat,' I say.

'But you must! You look worn out, Frankie. After the evening we've had, we're both worn out. We both need some soup.'

'Mum!' I've never made so much noise. I want to fill the whole flat, the block, the Estate, even the whole world.

She stops, finally. They say that just before you die your life flashes in front of you. There's even an old black-and-white film about it. *Owl Creek* or something like that. I saw it last year. This man is being lynched. He's on a bridge and they're going to drop him over the side, not into the water, but into nothing, because it's a lynching. They're hanging him and as he's plummeting down towards the tightening noose, he relives his life at top speed. That's what the film is about: how things might have been different for him, because, of course, he imagines that he escapes the noose.

That's what it feels like to me. Mum's standing there with the tin-opener jammed into the can but not turned; she's waiting, at last, for *me* to say something. It's as though we can't put it off any longer. All the things in the world that I *could* say to her are flashing through my mind. I could say what I think about Ian, about her awful campaign, about the gypsies, about Sam and what his stepbrothers have done to him. I could say it all. I could even tell her how I feel about Emilia. I know that at this moment I can make her listen. But I don't say any of that. I don't even bother to contradict her. I don't tell her that I'm *not* standing by her any more. When I open my mouth I say something quite different.

'I want to meet my grandma. I want to *know* her, Mum.'

She swallows down her gasp of outrage, then starts to turn the key of the opener. We both watch it slice the metal apart, watch the orangey red begin to drip.

'You can't do that, Francis.' She's speaking carefully.

'Why not? Is she dead?'

'No! Not her! She's–'

'What?'

Mum shrugs and doesn't meet my eye. Her lips are squeezed tight together. She thinks she's shut me up.

'What's she like then?'

Mum comes towards me with the opened can in her hand. I'm wondering if she's about to throw it in my face, like they do in films. Only that would be a bit much, wouldn't it, with tomato? But I'll risk it.

'Are you like her?'

'No! I am not!'

'Am I?'

Mum hesitates.

'No, of course not.'

'So why can't we meet?'

'Because . . . ' She turns her back to me and begins to stir. 'All right. Go and meet her, Frankie. I always knew you would, one day. But don't ask me to come, because I won't. Never. Now, do you want this soup or not?'

'No! Don't you understand? I don't want your bloody soup!'

'You don't have to shout,' she says primly.

'I *do*, Mum. I do have to shout!' I can hear my own voice

154

going out of control. 'What's wrong with you, Mum? All you ever say is "won't" and "don't" and "never". You're so wrong about everything and so blind. You said Ian was the one with his head in the sand but it's not true. It's *you*. You're the ostrich! You're so ignorant but you can't stop telling people what to do!'

I can't stop either. I know how awful I must sound, but I'm not going to shut up now. It's all too late. Sam's hurt. And other people too. If I don't speak now, my chance will go and my courage.

'This whole thing, Mum, this space not race thing, it's a nightmare and you've made it. It's in *your* head. You've made it all up and now it's causing all this fear and aggro and people are getting hurt. Like Sam . . . and . . . and Mrs Seagrove's Ernie. It's the same nightmare. Don't you care?' I know I haven't explained myself well, but she's heard me.

'You wouldn't understand, Francis. You're too young. It's not like that at all.'

'For heaven's sake, Mum–'

'Excuse me.' Lucy cautiously puts her head round the kitchen door. She pushes her hair out of her mouth and smiles unsteadily. Her lips are stretched so tight from ear to ear they look as if they'll crack open.

'I'm so sorry,' she whispers. 'I don't want to get in the way or anything. Or hear. Not that I have, honestly.' Her eyes are darting between us.

'I didn't eavesdrop, I promise. Even when Dad was here. It's just–' she snatches back the sodden clump, chews quickly, then spits it out again. 'It's just that I think Dad may have forgotten me.' She laughs a small unhappy laugh. Suddenly, for the first time I'm sorry for her. I really, truly am. And all the beastly things I've said and done come back to me.

'I'll take you home,' I offer. 'You can't go on your own. It's almost midnight.'

'There's no need,' says Mum.

'No, honestly.' Lucy is biting her lip. 'I can catch the late bus. I don't want to be a nuisance. Ever!'

'You're not,' I say. 'And I don't mind at all.' I take my jacket from the hook and we step out into the cold.

'I'm sure Ian didn't forget,' I say.

'Are you?' she asks bitterly.

I don't dare reply.

I meet Mrs Seagrove on my way back. She says that Snowy's missing again so she's searching the car park. I kneel down and peer under everything although I can't imagine why she'd stay outside here on a night like this. Frost is already glistening on car windows and my ears are burning with cold. Mrs Seagrove is wearing two hats.

'Snowy! Snowy! Snowy!' I must look a right prat, but I don't care.

'Snowy! Snowy! Snowy!' At least this stops me thinking about what I've got to do next.

'I don't trust anyone,' she says unexpectedly. 'Not after what I've seen tonight. That poor, poor lad!'

'So you *were* there, Mrs Seagrove.'

'Of course I was, with my friend Peg, what lives opposite, over the shops. But I didn't see you. I saw your mum, but not you.'

'I wasn't with Mum.'

She nods as though she hadn't expected me to be and I'm glad. Then I hear a miaow. It seems to come from her house.

'That's Snowy.' We look around the tiny front room but she's not there. I go into the hall.

'It can't be Snowy,' she says. But it is. When I open the door into the kitchen Snowy runs up to her and pushes against her legs. She doesn't seem that pleased, doesn't bend down to stroke the cat, but stares around her kitchen, and frowns.

'Now how did she get in there?' she asks, in a little puzzled voice.

I'm not surprised at all. The back door is wide open and the kitchen is full of cold night air.

'Maybe you forgot the door,' I suggest, 'when you went out.'

'Forget to shut my own back door? Never! I'm not in my second childhood. Not yet. Am I?'

I don't reply, but bolt the door, top and bottom, and turn the key. She's still looking around her kitchen, still wondering what's been nicked. That's what it's like in Poet's Rise.

'Mrs Seagrove?' I have to take a chance. 'What happened on the troopship?'

'Nobody knows,' she replies, 'not for sure. Not even me.' She shakes her head, looks round the kitchen one more time, then shuts the door. In the front room she settles herself and Snowy on the sofa and then looks up at me. 'When they went to take him his meal one evening, he was dead. He'd died there all alone with the door still locked and himself half under the sea. Died from the kicking, Mr Jones said, without him ever seeing a doctor. After all, he was only a gypsy, wasn't he?'

'Then?'

'He was "buried at sea", wasn't he? That's what they call

157

it.' She's speaking quite calmly. 'It must have been over the rails, mustn't it, in one of those bags? That's what Mr Jones said.'

'"A wicked waste of a fine young man",' I quote.

She nods.

'But you said that he was afraid of the sea, that he had to be on land!' As soon as it's out of my mouth I wish I'd kept quiet.

'It's all right,' she says and touches my hand. 'I used to worry about that too. Worried myself sick, if you want the truth. I used to worry about him over all those years, with him having no place to rest. It upset me so bad I had to go to the doctor myself about my nerves, but he couldn't do anything. Then one day when I was down by the sea, buying a bit of fish, to tell you the truth, I got to thinking about how the land doesn't just stop there, where the waves begin, does it? It goes on under the sea. I mean, how else did they build that tunnel to France? They showed that on the telly, and that's when I was sure that in the end, he would have some place to rest. There must have been some place somewhere, on some distant shore that was for him. Mustn't there?'

'Yes. There must have been.'

She nods again, and pats my hand.

'Lock up after me,' I say as I go, and I wait a second on the step, until I hear that she has. Because she's right, isn't she? You can't trust anyone, ever.

19

....

Tuesday 22 December

'You like?' Emilia asks over my shoulder in her voice of trampled leaves.

'Yes – no – yes,' I gabble. 'These pictures are . . . brilliant . . . but so sad, so–' I'm shaking my head and frowning. I don't mean to. It's just that I want her to understand how I feel.

'You *no* like.' Her smile is fading. It's as though a wind has blown through my heart and swept the leaves along the ground.

'I *like*, Emi. Honestly. I like.' That's what we call her now, Emi, and that's how we all speak too. I know it's daft but we still do it. She's just so special. Everybody feels it now and not just me. It's almost as though we've been waiting for her. I can't explain it at all except to admit that things are different, with her here. She behaves differently too. Look how she's treated me. Other girls might have got really worked up about that misunderstanding in the art room. But she didn't. She doesn't hold a grudge at all. She still smiles at me and she's never said anything. Not an unkind word.

This is the third time I've been back to look at Mrs Morris's exhibition. Yesterday I came early. There were hardly any teachers in school. It was just the cleaners and me, so I had to wait for them to unlock the library. As soon as I saw the pictures I understood why everyone is talking about them. They aren't just the Morrises' holiday snaps, though those are interesting and show how beautiful Romania is. Year 10 had done bits of Eastern Europe for a geography project and have made a relief map of Romania which is on display. Places of special interest are marked by little flags. You can see where Ceausescu built his palace and where he and his wife were shot. Then there are dots representing the Roma or gypsy villages. Ceausescu had these bulldozed to the ground. There's even a flag stuck in the hometown of that famous girl gymnast, Nadia something or other, and there's another for Count Dracula and the valleys in Transylvania where the vampires are supposed to come from. It's very interesting.

Mrs Morris has assembled dozens of books about gypsies, and not just about those in Romania. There are groups of gypsies scattered all over the world, even in America, which I didn't know. I also didn't know about Hitler and the Nazis.

One of the books has photographs showing a picture of the huts where gypsies were held in concentration camps in the Second World War. Underneath it said that Hitler's scientists first experimented with their poison gases on the gypsies. It made me feel really odd reading all that, and I wondered whether such books should be there and whether it wouldn't be too frightening for little kids like Lucy. It is *so* gross.

I was quite glad to get on to the section about gypsies in

160

Britain and the hop-picking. People had brought in all sorts of stuff from their relatives. When I went the second time I spent ages looking at these photos. Some of them were taken before the war so I tried to examine the faces in case one was of Mrs Seagrove's Ernie. Apparently, in a church in Hadlow, which isn't so far from here, there's a memorial to gypsies. In 1853 there was an accident on the bridge as the hop-pickers returned across the River Medway. One of their wagons overturned into the water and thirty people were drowned. One family, the Leatherlands, lost sixteen people. 1853: that's about a hundred and fifty years ago, isn't it? It makes you think.

Yesterday I went round to Mrs Seagrove after I'd been to the exhibition. I'm sure she'll be interested and I'd like to take her, though maybe I ought to try and hide the nasty bits from her. She wasn't in, when I knocked, so I'll go again this evening. It won't be till later because I have to see Sam first.

He's going to be all right and can have visitors now. Miss Chester announced this in Assembly. She didn't do prayers for him but she made this great speech. She said she was proud of him because he'd been standing up for what is right. 'Biting for what's right', Arshad had whispered to me. I nearly choked but actually I thought it was very decent of the Axe to say all that, and I wished that Mum could have heard her.

Yasmina has already visited Sam. She and Mrs Rushmore went yesterday on behalf of our tutor group. She says his spleen was damaged when they kicked him. The doctor told her that people can easily die from those injuries because sometimes nobody notices or believes that they've been

161

badly hurt. I nodded when Yasmina told us this, but I don't *actually* know where the spleen is. I'll ask about it in PSE. It'll make a change from those endless questions about oral sex. The girls always ask those to embarrass the teacher. It'll be nice to have something useful to talk about. After all, folks around here are always getting a kicking, but I don't actually see much sign of the other, despite what all the lads say in the changing rooms.

The three of us, me, Yasmina and Emi are still looking at the pictures when Mrs Morris comes in after lunch. Emi is chattering away. It's her sort of English but with Romanian and bits of her Roma dialect thrown in. I don't follow at all and I don't think Mrs Morris does either, but Yasmina explains that Emi is describing where she used to live. I can't see how Yasmina has worked that out, but it doesn't matter either. I just like to be near Emi. Today she has red slides in her hair, red plastic slides, shaped like flowers. She's much tidier since she's been living with the Morris family. She still doesn't wear the proper uniform but actually other people don't either. And she always looks nice. Or beautiful, even. I don't know what it is, exactly, because lots of girls are prettier, but there's something about Emi. There's something in her face that I keep wanting to look at. It's like the sea: you can look at it for ever, people say. I want to look at her like that. Then, when I'm with her, I hardly look at her at all.

Now I've gone back to examine one of the pictures more closely. It's a drawing and it's very, very complicated. From a distance you might think that the whole surface of the paper is covered in scribbles. Close up it's a landscape or cityscape. That's what the label says. I think it's by one of the teachers in the art department. Maybe he went to Romania for his hols. It must be the in thing for teachers at the moment. It's probably dirt cheap, that's why.

This drawing has been done with thousands and thousands of marks and lines. It's an odd thing to work with, because you can't rub it out can you? No chance for second thoughts. It's a bit like the drawings Sam does, only much more complicated. Maybe Sam gets his ideas from this teacher, because this particular picture is pretty much like the one that was up on the board. It's just better.

'You *like*?' Emi asks again.

This time I nod and grin. She smiles at me.

'That's good thing.' It's another of her favourite sayings, that and 'OK'. She can speak a whole language with 'OK.'

'Mr Bresslaw says he's going to take some of these pictures to show his wife,' says Yasmina. I nearly say something rude but I don't. It's not Yasmina's fault that she doesn't know about my mum and Ian Bresslaw. I just ask why.

'His wife's some artist–'

'I know that!'

'Why are you asking then?' Yasmina looks at me.

'What I meant is, *why* does Ian's wife want to see this guy's pictures?'

'It isn't a *guy*, you idiot.'

'OK. Woman, then.'

'It isn't a woman, either.' Yasmina's eyes are twinkling.

'You mean it's a student?'

'It's Emi, you idiot.'

'*Emi*?' I don't understand. Or do I?

'Yes! Oh, don't tell me you didn't know, Frankie! Everybody knows. How can you be so blind?'

'You mean these are *her* drawings?'

'Yes. Obviously.' Yasmina is pointing to Emilia's name.

'But . . . ' I don't say it. I stop myself just in time, although it was there and almost out of my mouth. I hate myself for even knowing how to think such things.

The only safe place to look is at the drawings again. So I do. At *her* pictures. She's drawn a building that I almost know: a mean, high, rotting block, with balconies and doors that will not close. Poky windows open from damp, dark rooms upon views that are of nothing at all. She's scrawled it, more than drawn it, and I don't mean that in a nasty way. What I mean is that the biro in her hand must have gone so fast. And so confidently. She's looked up at this grey concrete monster and felt some sort of fear. You can tell that right away, even though washing still hangs on its balconies and people in rooms are watching TV. I look more closely. Then I see the flames: red biro flames, like little, eager tongues. Then I see that that is why, at one corner, so many people are on the balcony. They are crowded together, crushing each other.

And that's why there is another crowd of people on the ground, looking up. It's not our block at all. I've made a mistake. She never meant to draw Poet's Rise. She has been drawing from memories of her home. In her representation one figure has leapt from the balcony. Or fallen. Who can tell? With arms outstretched and skirts blown up above her waist like fatal, useless wings, her mouth is open and her hands held out as though she is surprised at what is happening to her. As though she didn't expect it.

It's late when I finally get to Mrs Seagrove's flat again. I only spent ten minutes with Sam because other people were there and I couldn't ask him anything special or private. In fact we didn't say much at all. Just *hi*, and then I sat on this plastic chair by his bed and tried not to stare. I've never seen him look clean. People from school were there and they were mucking about with his fruit. They were cranking his bed up and down and listening to the hospital radio, so I don't think he noticed when I left. He hardly noticed that I'd been. Then it took ages and ages on the bus.

I've knocked on Mrs Seagrove's door. Now I'm tapping on the window. There's no reply. Snowy's inside. She's jumped up on the window ledge and is rubbing her nose against the glass as if she's pleased to see me and would like me to come in.

I knock once more, then leave. It's too cold to hang around.

Mum isn't in either. She's been and gone, by the look of the dirty plates left in the sink. We've hardly spoken these last two days. This must be like the run-up to divorce because it's exactly how people at school describe it. First their parents begin to lead separate lives, then they stop talking to each other. Then one fine day it's 'sit down dear, we've something to tell you' time. I wish. Actually, I think children should be able to divorce their parents. It'd be great.

Later, in the night, I hear something. I know I have. Suddenly, I'm awake again. It *was* something. It's gone now, but it was there. I get out of bed and go into the front room.

I can't see anything. The curtains, Mum's new green velvet curtains, haven't been drawn. Cold air from the night beyond drifts across the room and touches my face. I stand close to the window and slowly wipe the condensation from the glass. A quiet night after all.

'Frankie?' Mum is curled up in the corner of the sofa. She's made me jump but I didn't show it. I wipe the glass again. The water trickles down my wrist. There *is* someone in the car park. And why not? It is almost Christmas. Some people go out and celebrate.

'Can you see them?' she whispers eagerly.

'See who?' I ask before I can stop myself.

'Those gypsies – and before you start, Francis, I just happened to see them when I was coming in. So I *know* it's them down there now.'

'What are you talking about?' I ask roughly, hoping my tone will shut her up.

'It *is* those gypsies, Frankie. I *know* they're down there. Aren't they?'

'How should I know? And so what?'

'Nothing. I'm just saying. But they're acting suspiciously.'

I press my face against the glass. I want to see for myself: to prove her wrong. I force open the balcony door and step out on to the freezing concrete. Then I lean over and call out. Don't ask me why. I feel foolish as soon my feeble little 'hey' drifts down. But there *are* people down there. They call briefly, sharply to each other. Then they run. They tear out of the car park and into the High Street, where they split up. I hate to admit it, but it looks pretty suspicious. Still, that's nothing new for Poet's Rise.

'Why do you think it was the gypsies?' Back inside I'm struggling to keep my voice very calm, very casual.

'I *know* it was.' Mum's voice is smug.

Our shabby old carpet feels as soft and warm as silk to my bare feet. I swallow nervously.

'Mum . . . can I ask something?'

'Well–'

I'm glad I can't see her face. Her mouth will be buttoned up, her pop eyes bulging defensively.

'Mum, this stuff about the gypsies, you know, the way you feel about . . . the . . . problem. *Why* do you feel like this?'

'I just do. Everybody does really, don't they?'

'Do they?' I struggle to make my voice innocent.

'Oh yes. You're too young to understand properly, but you only have to look at the way they live: always wandering about and not knowing how to live in proper houses.' Her voice is reaching out to me, trying to draw me close, trying to make me think like she does.

'Mum, where did you get your ideas about gypsies and . . . other people?'

'Actually,' she laughs a tinny little laugh, 'I hate to admit it after all I've said about her, but it's from my mother. Your grandma, who you're suddenly so keen to see.'

'She didn't like–'

'No! Couldn't stand them. Nor the Irish! Lazy, that's what she always said the Irish were, charming, but lazy. So there's no way you can call her a racist, either. She just used to speak her mind, and still does, I dare say. She has her faults, or else we wouldn't have fallen out with each other, would we? But she was right about some things.'

' "Right?" ' I feel as though I'm back in that alley, groping my way through things I can't bear to touch. 'So you and your mum are quite alike?'

'Me and Mother? Alike? Rubbish! Whatever gave you that idea?' I sense that she's staring at me through the darkness. Her voice is low.

'My mother is a very *difficult* woman, Francis. If you'd met her, you'd understand.'

We are silent. I wait. I hear her draw in a deep breath and I dread what she'll say next.

'Maybe,' she falters, 'maybe you *should* meet her, luv. I've been thinking about what you said the other night. Maybe it's time. Maybe I've been a bit hasty. Shall I fix something up?'

I want to say no. I want to scream it. I want to tell her that I don't care any longer. It's too late. There's no gentle, thoughtful old soul waiting for me with trembling hands and an old-fashioned, checked dress. There's just another stupid bigoted woman who will disappoint me just as much. I don't think I can bear that.

I stretch stiffly and put my weight against the balcony door. It's almost shut, but I can feel a draught like a blade. It must be bitter out there. I wonder briefly where Sam's father is on a night like this. Is he out there too? It makes me shiver. What must it be like to have the door of the family home shut in one's face?

And suddenly I wish that that had happened to me. That Mum had left me out on a step in the night. And that I'd been found, and brought into some other warmer place.

20

....

Tuesday night

'Francis!' Mrs Morris calls as I hurry past the library. I overslept again and shouldn't stop now, but I do.

'Francis, have you got a minute?' She's smiling at me and I can smell her perfume. 'It's about the Christmas disco tonight.' She's scrutinizing my face. Can she hear my heart begin to race? 'We just wondered, Katy and me, when we were talking last night, whether you'd like to come with us?'

'With you?'

'Yes. If you'd like to. If you're not already going with anyone else. We just wondered, and thought it would be nice. You could join our table.' She's watching me. What she really means is, join 'the enemy'. 'We could pick you up from Poet's Rise, or you could come to supper first. It's nothing special: just snacks with me and my husband, and Katy of course and her dad. And Emi. A couple of her special friends are coming too. And you. If you'd like to.'

Would I like to? Would I ever! I could have kissed her, worked for ever in her library, or waltzed her right around it, except that I don't know how to waltz. I'll do anything for

169

her, after this. Is this what winning the lottery is like, or finally making a film, or finishing first in a marathon, when you've always been the one at the back? It's like a dream come true, or better, because my dreams always end on waking. This is better, because it's life.

I stumble into English late. I can't concentrate on anything. Mrs Rushmore blows me up and I don't mind at all. Then I get a detention when she finds I haven't done the homework. I smile at her, I can't think of anything but the coming evening and of Emi. I don't really believe that she'll be there, that she'll step out of the Morrises' front door with Katy and me, and the others too, chattering and laughing and all dressed up. Will we really cram ourselves into the back of that car with the leather seats? If we do, I'll have to take care not to squash her. I wouldn't want to spoil her dress. I know she'll be wearing something special, because all the girls will be. They've talked about nothing else all week. Vicky Jackson's dress is gold, she told us, and very low cut. Big deal. Arshad sniggered that anybody who's interested in what Vicky Jackson has will have already seen it. Mark choked, but I thought, so what?

I'm only interested in Emi. I picture her stepping out of the house. She'll be wearing red. It'll be a very dark red and silky and shiny against her pale, freckled skin. This evening her hair won't be in plaits. Mrs Morris and Katy will have helped her do it up on the top of her head. She'll look quite grown up. She could even have gone to a hairdresser's, couldn't she? And Mrs Morris will have lent her a necklace. It will sparkle around her throat.

I'll ask her to dance. She won't want to, not at first. So I'll reassure her. I'll demonstrate that I can't dance either and it doesn't matter. Nobody young knows how to dance properly any more. It's no good. She'll still hang back. It's understandable isn't it? This must all be so very different from what she's used to. She'll want to stand behind the others, so I'll stay with her, watching and chatting, until she's more at ease. But in the end, I'll persuade her. She'll give in. I'll lead her to a quiet part of the dance floor. I'll hold her hand. She'll come to me and put her bare arms around my neck. The dark red dress will rustle as I step closer. Her face will be near mine. I'll tell her things. People will begin to watch us. They'll draw a little apart, to give us room to dance. And we will. Somehow, she and I will dance. The music will go even quieter. I'll half realize that we are all alone on the floor and that everybody is watching us, admiring us. She'll murmur my name in that voice of hers and she'll almost close her eyes, so she won't realize that we are the centre of attention. But I do. I'll put my arm more firmly around her and when I hold her close she won't pull away.

At lunchtime I remember that I haven't got a clean shirt. I know that Arshad and his dad are wearing DJs, but it'll have to be black jeans for me and my new denim shirt. If I dash home now I can hand them both in at the launderette and pick them up on the way home. It'll be worth it. Lucy told me ages ago that I looked really good in black.

I see the police cars and the ambulance as soon as I reach the car park. A whole area is taped off. It doesn't seem like a normal break-in inquiry. The watching crowd is too silent. There is no shrieking family trying to claw back the guy being dragged off for questioning – and it always is a guy.

'What's happening?' I ask someone.

'They've broken into that old woman's flat now, the one with that white cat.'

'Not Mrs Seagrove? What's happened to her?'

'Well she's dead, isn't she? That's what everyone's saying. I never knew her name, poor old girl. Sea – what did you say?'

'Seagrove.' I can barely speak. 'Mrs Seagrove. Are you sure about this?' I feel sick. It's like *I've* been kicked too, right in my stomach, even though it probably isn't true. This place is full of rumour. Why would anyone want to kill Mrs Seagrove? 'She can't be dead.' I protest. 'I knocked on her door yesterday. I saw her cat through the window.'

'Well, perhaps you'd better tell the police, love, they're asking for information. Only *I* don't know anything. I didn't even know her name. You don't do you, with all the comings and goings there are on this estate. Poor old thing, what a way to go. Been dead some time, people are saying, only nobody knew until her cat wouldn't stop carrying on.'

'Who did it? Do they know?' For some reason I'm whispering. The woman whispers back.

'A few people are saying that it was those gypsies. Some woman saw them hanging around last night. I mean, I don't know anything about it. But that's what people are saying. I'm only repeating it. Wicked, isn't it?'

I don't actually believe it. I can't think about it at all. It could still be a mistake. People are always saying dumb stuff like this around here.

I get my clothes from the flat and hand them in. They're already discussing the 'murder' at the launderette. I don't want to listen so I hurry out. Back at school everyone knows. It's been on the lunch-time news. Her back door was forced. Mrs Seagrove was shut up in the cupboard in the hall, then left. Locked in, and left while they ransacked the flat. Cause of death hasn't been established, the bulletin said, but the police are following up several leads from local people.

I can't even remember there being a cupboard in the hall. We haven't got one – only the one for the meters. They couldn't mean that, surely?

There's an odd atmosphere in class. It's almost the end of term and Christmas too. Then there's the disco, and now this. No one can keep quiet. We can't concentrate. It's horrible and funny at the same time, like some awful movie. I ask you: shut up in a cupboard! It's grotesque; that's the word for it. Several people laughed. And I did too. I couldn't help it.

Just before the lesson began Arshad and one of the lads shut Mona in the stationery room. It was only for a second but boy, did she scream! They were hauled off to see the Axe, but we'd all howled hysterically. I don't think they meant it so badly. They just didn't think. I can't either.

I don't know how one can think about something like this. Sam was bad enough, but this? This is sick. And I'm afraid. I'm afraid that I *could have* done something. I should have, shouldn't I, when I saw Snowy on the windowsill? I should have done something then. Or even before. On that night when the back door was open. Maybe that was the beginning. Maybe someone had been in then. I should have done more than bolt the door.

I ought to have gone to the police then and I must go now. I've got stuff to tell them, but not yet. Not until after this evening. It won't make any difference, will it? It's too late to do any good. Worry is making my head ache. That, and the noise in class.

'*Shut up!*' Mrs Rushmore is screaming herself. It's so unlike her we all fall silent instantly. She goes red. Vicky takes a chance:

'Please miss,' she lisps in her phoney little girl's voice, 'can we go home early if there's a murderer about?'

Mrs Rushmore finally loses her rag. She yells at Vicky so loudly that Ian, who happens to be next door, comes in and has a word. It's agreed that if we're quiet, seriously quiet, we can have free time until the bell goes. Mrs Rushmore gathers up her papers and flees. I feel quite put out: she's abandoned us. I don't want to do much, but the rest of the class does. They want to talk about what's happened in Poet's Rise.

I look at Emi. She's drawing busily. She hasn't understood anything. Yasmina is sitting beside her. With Sam still away she's always there. The muttered word 'murder' rustles through the class. People are mentioning gypsies too. Emi bends over her paper. One or two girls are sniffing back tears now and talking about their grannies, and how it could happen to them too. I don't feel like crying, though perhaps I should. After all, I actually knew her. I suppose she was almost a friend. Mark, who's from Poet's Rise too, says that he knew the old girl really well. She was always going on at him about her cat. She used to accuse him of trying to steal it. He did once, but only for a joke. He thought she was a bit touched. Vicky flares up again when he says this. Being a bit touched isn't a reason to bump anyone off, she shouts. Ian bangs on the wall. Mark mutters that he didn't *mean* that. Mrs Rushmore comes back, looking a bit sheepish. She joins in the chat but warns us about not jumping to conclusions. Nobody knows what really happened, she says.

'I do,' Vicky hisses, under her breath. Then she says something about gypsies.

Yasmina turns round and glares at Vicky, but nobody meets her eye. Mrs Rushmore is suddenly very busy with her papers. In the sudden, uncomfortable lull I notice that everyone is looking over to where Emilia sits and draws. I want the bell to go. I want this to end.

I meet Liz Quiggley on the stairs. I'd like to ask about Sam but don't. We pass without a word. Mum isn't back yet. At least that's good. Perhaps I can get out of here without seeing her. I'm not asking her for money for my ticket. I took some from my savings account on the way home. I don't want anything from Mum at all. Just that she doesn't come back. My clothes look fine. I felt so awkward crossing the car park with them swinging brightly from hangers, when this hideous thing has happened down there. I run the water for a bath. I'll have to be quick. I glance down from the balcony. Part of the car park is still taped off. A few people are still standing around. Mum *couldn't* have seen anything from up here. No way. And in the dark. So she wouldn't have said anything to the police. She couldn't.

I'm dressed too soon; the shirt and jeans feel very clean and ironed, but I look OK. Despite dawdling I arrive far too early. I hardly ever come to this part of the town. It's nearer than I thought, but still a world away. It even smells different. The houses are set back from the road and there are gardens with old trees and iron gates in front. The High Street climate of chips and curry, spilt beer and bus exhaust has stayed back there with the flashing Christmas lights and

175

tacky, tinkling tunes. Here, I glimpse lit trees in the corners of living rooms and wreaths with real holly and ribbons, hanging on nicely painted front doors. I bet the kids in this street hang up old-fashioned woolly socks and almost believe in Father Christmas, even after they're quite grown up.

The Morrises have a Christmas tree. I can see it through the opened curtains and they are standing around it. I don't see Emi but it doesn't matter. I know she'll be there. And I can't see anyone in a DJ. It's a relief. I want Emi to think how smart I look, not notice that I'm out of step with everyone else. I untuck my shirt. Now it hides my backside which I worry about, though I also worry that the shirt makes me look a bit like a tent. Still, everybody says it's personality which counts. And I have got a personality. She'll recognize that when we get talking. I'll tell her things and not just while we're dancing.

I'll tell her that I've been learning all this stuff about gypsies and that I really do understand how difficult it must be for her to start a new life here. I'll tell her how much I admire what she's done in leaving her family. I'll say that I'm sure she misses them, no, maybe not that. People in school have told me that she doesn't ever want to go back to them, that she's always dreamed of going to a school and then training to be an artist. Gypsy girls never do stuff like that normally. So perhaps it's safer not to talk about her family, just to tell her that I'm her friend, that she can always rely on me. Then, I must talk about myself. That's important. You have to tell people about stuff that *you've* done. Shakespeare does that in *Othello*. He makes Desdemona fall in love with Othello because of the wonderful

176

stories he told her about his life and adventures as a sea captain:

> She loved me for the dangers I had pass'd,
> And I loved her that she did pity them.
> This only was the witchcraft I have used.

Those are the lines from *Othello*. I often think about them. And they're still true. Other people's worlds come alive when they talk about them, don't they? Like Mrs Seagroves.' Like lies. They come alive too. Some people will believe anything, even huge, obvious whoppers. But I shan't lie. Not to Emi.

I've walked up and down this street twice. It's only just after six, but I'll have to go in. I must look suspicious and I'm freezing.

'Frankie!' A car slows down. It's Yasmina. Her parents wave as they drop her off. She's transformed, almost unrecognizable. It's her national dress, I suppose, and those thick black lines around her eyes make her look different. She's more an exotic bird than a girl, in that brilliant dress.

'Wow!' I can't help it. She laughs and twirls round and round on the pavement outside. It was her mother's, she says, and she's only put it on for a laugh. Normally Yasmina wears jeans.

'Well, come on then, Frankie. They're not going to eat you!' She takes my arm. How does she know? I shrug and let her drag me up the gravel drive.

Emi isn't in the room. Katy says she isn't just shy, she's anxious. Her uncle and father have been round twice today.

They're trying to persuade her to come back to them. She hasn't, but it's upset her. She's afraid they may be waiting outside and will make a scene.

'I didn't see anyone,' I say. Katy nods. She's relieved. Mr Morris shakes my hand. Mrs Morris gives me a Christmas kiss and a glass of something which I gulp straight down. At the last moment, as we are piling into the car, Emi runs from the house and squeezes in beside Katy.

Mr Morris brakes sharply as we turn into the school car park. We tumble about in the back and Mrs Morris tells him to watch what he's doing. Then we see that the entrance has been blocked. Someone has dragged a couple of wheelie bins across. Part of the huge poster advertising the charity disco has been torn down.

'I don't like the look of this.' Mr Morris tries to reverse but can't. A line of other cars has built up behind. Someone approaches and taps on the window. Katy begins to wind it down. Her father shouts at her not to. There are a lot of people standing around in the car park. I can hear music very faintly, so it must have begun.

'Sorry about this, luv.' Some bloke leans against the car in a chatty fashion. 'There ain't going to be no bloody disco! Not to help no murdering gypsies. Not on your life.'

Mrs Morris is about to leap out of the car and tell him off. This time Katy shrieks 'no'. Then we're very quiet. We've got his message. He nods and ambles off to the car behind. A group of sixth-formers are approaching on foot. In the road horns start to blast impatiently. The students begin to argue. Some of them are trying to shove their way through. One of the big blokes pushes back his balaclava as he squares up to take a swing and I recognize Alan Quiggley, one of Sam's stepbrothers. Then I see Barry. He's standing in the lit-up entrance to the school hall. I can seen the decorations, the Christmas tree and the students dressed up in their very best behind him. He has his arms spread out. He's keeping people in and at the same time he's trying to fend off those outside. He's leaping from side to side like some mad goalkeeper. He's doing OK.

'Emi! Don't! Stay where you are!' We all scream at once.

She doesn't. She opens the door and is out, out in the road in the glare of the headlights. I grab at her as she leaves the car. I catch at the sleeve of her coat and cling on but she pulls free. Now, as she stands there, the coat drops to the ground. She's looking from side to side. She takes one step. Her red velvet skirt sweeps the road. This time her feet aren't bare; this time she's wearing little slipper things that shine gold in the lights.

'There's one of them!' someone yells. But it isn't just anyone. It's Liz. Of course. '*There* she is!'

Katy and I are already out of the car. Emi begins to run.

'Stop! Emi, don't run. Stop!'

But she doesn't. And why should she, even if she could understand? She's seen it all before, hasn't she? She's seen the hunt, and the buildings torched. She's seen a young girl jump.

'Emilia!'

We're trying to get to her, but she's darting to and fro and the others are closing in. As she moves, her plaits swing wildly from side to side.

Liz steps in front of her and opens her arms wide. And grins with satisfaction. Emi stops.

'No!' We've seen the blade. Liz catches hold of those ropes

of hair and pulls Emilia in. She drags the girl towards her, step by step. A hand is raised, then slashes down, once, then twice, and cuts right through. Emilia doesn't move. In the crowd a woman laughs. Emi puts her hand up to the back of her head and touches the place, touches where the hair is all cut off.

'So you think you can come over here and hurt old ladies, do you?' jeers Liz. 'Well, you *can't*! So you'd better go back where you belong, before you really get hurt!'

A man gets to Emi before I can. He takes her by the elbow and holds her very tight. I try to reach her, I really do. I try, but I can't stop him from leading her away.

'Do something,' I beg. 'Please!'

'We can't.' Mrs Morris puts an arm around my shoulders. 'He's her father.'

'And I'm her friend . . . '

But nobody hears me amongst the chaos of the night.

21

Tuesday 5 January 1999

Now people are saying that it was some kids from Milton House, further down on Poet's Rise. Some were quite little kids, about Lucy's age, actually. I think one is in her tutor group. They never intended to kill Mrs Seagrove, not to murder her. No way. Or even to hurt her. And it wasn't murder, anyway, and not really a killing, because they never hurt her, did they? They didn't even knock her about. They couldn't help it, could they, if the old dear just went and died? She must have had a weak heart, mustn't she? In fact she probably did. And was soft in the head. Anybody could see that. After all, she often wore two hats at the same time. That's what the parents around here are saying.

It was a . . . joke. A laugh. It was a bit of acting up that went wrong. All boys act up, now and again, don't they? And what's more the old girl didn't put herself out to be nice. If she wasn't exactly asking for trouble, she was still a mean, twisted old stick. Look how she always carried on about her precious cat. Hadn't she picked on those boys, accusing them of doing nasty things to it? Which was sick of her. Sick. And they never did. No way. They are all animal

181

lovers. They watch all the TV programmes about animal hospitals. One of the families kept five dogs in their flat until the neighbours complained and the RSPCA were called out.

That's what people around here are saying. As for me, I don't know. I don't know anything any longer, only that Emi is gone, and not just from school and the Morrises. She's gone right away and for ever. I know I should only be thinking about Mrs Seagrove, because that's the real thing, isn't it, death? You need to think about it. But I don't. I start off thinking about her and it but before I know it, I'm back thinking about Emi. Who is alive after all. But gone.

She never even came back for her things, for all those new clothes and stuff, and the paints that the Morrises had bought for her: the first box of paints, the *only* box of paints she'd ever had. Katy says that other people had given her loads of presents: strangers even sent little parcels after the local newspaper had printed an article about her. All those gifts were piled up under the Christmas tree waiting for her, but she never came back.

Mr Morris packed everything up into a suitcase and tried to give it to her father but he wouldn't take it, wouldn't even touch the handle of the case. He refused to have them in the room. Apparently the Roma think that the things are dirty now. 'Contaminated': that's the word Katy used.

She also told us that after her grandfather had brought the suitcase back he sat down in the kitchen and poured himself a drink and cried. She's never seen him so upset. It's odd, isn't it? People never cry over the worst things. They cry over stupid stuff like Christmas presents given back.

But I cry. In secret. And this morning it wasn't secret, it

was in school, in English. I couldn't stop. We were reading the last act in *Othello*. There's this bit at the end: Desdemona has been killed and Emilia refuses to keep quiet about the truth. She says:

'Twill out, 'twill out; I hold my peace sir? no;
No, I will speak as liberal as the north;
Let heaven, and men, and devils, let 'em all,
All, all, cry shame against me, yet I'll speak.

Then Iago tries to shut her up, tries to stop her letting the cat out of the bag. 'Be wise, and get you home.' That's what he says. And that's when I began to cry. The stabbing bit, where Iago strikes Emilia with his sword, hasn't even happened yet, and I'm sniffing pathetically, before it's even taken place. I said that it was because of Mrs Seagrove, but of course it wasn't. Mrs Rushmore asked Yasmina to take me down to the sick bay. On the way Yasmina told me to go to the doctor too, that it's not normal to cry like this. I suppose she's right because she's always so sensible, but I don't know if I'll go. I've always been sensible, haven't I? And look where it's got me.

It's just that I miss Emilia. It's just that she's not there, that she's *never* going to be, that I'm never, ever going to see her again, because they'll always move on, won't they? They'll always have to move on to someplace else, somewhere, anywhere, so long as it's far away from here. And she'll go too. Because what is there here?

People say that they took the last ferry across the Channel before Christmas, when it was already sleeting and the wind was getting up. Sometimes I think about her standing by the rails with that red skirt blown up and her feet in flip-flops again. I'm sure it would still be like that, even for a journey in winter.

I can't think about her face, except in dreams and that's not thinking, is it? Not really. I don't know what she looks like any more with her plaits cut off like that, with her neck white and exposed to the salty wind.

I hoped that if I came down here and sat where Mrs Seagrove and I sat that day, then I might be able to think about things properly. To sort of plan something, though I don't know what.

But I can't. I can't plan anything at all. It's just so cold. Even though I ran all the way and have only just sat down on the bench, I'm not at all warm.

Yesterday was the first day of the spring term, and nobody mentioned her name. They've taken the exhibition and all her pictures down. There's a display about bridges in the library. It's part of CDT and one of the classes has made a model out of matchsticks: thousands and thousands and thousands of matchsticks. It's pretty impressive, actually. I went to look at it with Arshad. He wants to be an engineer. But I don't. I don't want to be anything at all. Not ever. Not now. It doesn't seem as if there's anything worth doing.

I just don't understand how everyone can carry on as if nothing has happened. Even decent people, like old Barry. He was just the same this morning: trading insults with the lads, yelling at me to get a move on. Yet on the night of the disco he was a real hero, everyone said afterwards. He kept all the kids safe in the hall; he kept the thugs out. It could all have been a whole lot worse, people are saying now. I don't see it. But that's what they say. And today, he is just Barry again, with his red eyes and his stinking, beery breath.

'For chrissake Frankie, *move* it!' he yelled. And I did. I outran most of them but that was only because I didn't want them to see my face. Even though I could have said it was the wind that had made my eyes water. But I didn't. I just ran.

I don't know how Mum and I got through the Christmas holidays but we did. She's seeing some new bloke. I haven't met him yet, but I just get the feeling that he'll turn out to be another loser. Another Brian, knowing my luck. Still, that's her business, isn't it?

I actually miss old Ian. And Lucy. I never thought I would but I do. I could have done with sitting on the sofa and looking at her stupid magazines again. But Ian never came round to the flat again and I've heard that Lucy went back to the country to stay with her mother in that house along that unlit lane. I saw Ian a couple of times during the holidays. He was on his own, and buying meals for one in the supermarket. He nodded and asked how it was going and then he said something very strange indeed. It wasn't an Ian Bresslaw sort of thing at all.

'I know you don't believe me,' he said, looking at the beer stacked box on box, 'but I really cared about your mum.'

I didn't reply. I mean, whatever can you say to that? But he wouldn't shut up.

'And the thing is, Frankie, I still do. Despite everything, and all the things she's said and done, I still do. I know I shouldn't and I know it's no good, but I do, Frankie. And you can tell her that, if you get the chance. I've tried, but she won't listen to me. But I loved June–' Then he grabbed his trolley and dashed off.

I believe him. And I envy him too, because I don't love her any more. It's as if all that has withered away and died. I don't know how to do it any longer.

I can't even see Emilia's face now, except sometimes, and in dreams, and even then she's not looking at me. She's looking up at something else, something that I can't see at all.